TRY NOT TO DIE

In The

Shadowlands

ANDREW NAJBERG

VINCERE
P R E S S

Published by Vincere Press
65 Pine Ave., Ste 806
Long Beach, CA 90802

Printed in the United States of America
First Edition

ISBN: 9781961740273
Library of Congress Control Number: 2024921984

Front and back cover by Jun Ares
Edit by Mark Tullius and Horrorsmith Editing

Note From the Publisher

Try Not to Die: In The Shadowlands is the third book in the *TNTD* series that I haven't coauthored. After Jon Cohn impressed me with *Try Not to Die: On Slashtag*, I began thinking about other authors I'd trust to take on a *TNTD* book solo. It might be less fun for me, but it allows me to focus on growing the series while still contributing to some of the titles.

After reading *Gollitok* by Andrew Najberg, I knew I had to ask him to write one of these books. His writing immediately clicked with me—like Duncan Ralston, Cohn, and my other coauthors, I loved everything he wrote. So, I asked him to write a *TNTD* with no restrictions on subject matter.

Andrew submitted the manuscript just before we attended the Tennessee Books and Reader Convention. That plane trip was one of my favorites; I was so absorbed in the book, enjoying the characters, humor, brutal deaths, and the multiple endings. The rest of the weekend was equally fantastic with my table next to Andrew's. I was able to edit the manuscript and ask him questions, handing it back to him on Sunday.

This book also differs from others in that it doesn't include a survivor version. Andrew's writing makes this one of the most interactive books in the series, where decisions truly matter. A survivor version would rob readers of much of the story and fun.

So, I've made the first decision for you: read the interactive version. And be prepared to die. A lot. I hope you have as much fun doing it as I did.

Mark Tullius

Trigger Warning
...and a note about how to play this game

Dear Reader,

Thank you so much for venturing into The Shadowlands with Danny. Although I did not publish any writing in this world until 2023, its roots are nearly a decade old, and I'm so excited for people to finally have a chance to set foot in it through the page.

About this book—first and foremost: THIS IS NOT A CHILDREN'S BOOK.

If you've read *The Neverborn Thief*, please be aware that, unlike *Neverborn*, this book is meant to provide an adult readership an experience in The Shadowlands. Despite the relatively young age of its protagonist, it is bloody, violent, and explores serious, dark themes.

Warnings aside, if you're picking up a *Try Not to Die* book, then there is a good chance this is not your first and that you're well familiar with the format. However, if this *is*—and thank you for making this book your introduction—this book operates quite similar to many other choose your own adventure novels, much like the ones I grew up reading that made me aspire to one day write a book, just like this one. You'll come across regular branches in the story that ask you, the reader, to make key choices that determine how your story proceeds.

However, there is a key difference. Along the way, you're going to come across three choices that work a little differently. These choices will ask you to make record of the choice you made. Please, follow this faithfully—it will shape your overall read and determine which of eight endings you'll receive at the end of the book!

No matter how you choose to play it, thank you so much for playing! If, when you are done, you want to spend more time in

The Shadowlands, check out *The Neverborn Thief* and join twelve-year-old Connor Brighton in his attempt to navigate the perils of this otherworld.

Sincerely,
Andrew Najberg

To my family –
You are why I do what I do

Andrew

TRY NOT TO DIE
In The Shadowlands

The Last Beautiful Thing

For everything you do, there is a last time you will do it: a last time you enter your elementary school, the last time you call your mother "Mommy", the last time you go for a walk with your dad.

The last time you tell your little brother, "Yeah, you can go for a swim."

Sometimes, we see these through hindsight years down the road, when our lives have drifted in directions rendering repetitions of them impossible. But I recognize the last time I'll ever see something truly beautiful the exact moment it happens.

There, in front of me—what must be one thousand white roses, hundreds of chrysanthemums, forget-me-nots, lilies. Some in vases. Others wound into wreaths. There is music and crying. A woman in the front row moans. Air rattles in the vents blowing cold enough that my nose is wet with it.

Mom sits on the steps to the altar and gazes vacantly out to the crowd. Her hand moves like she is counting heads, but it is more like something she started and then simply forgot she was doing it.

There are too many people to count anyway. The chapel is full, and they're all in black. If I let my eyes sweep across them, I lose track of where one person ends and another begins. All those pink, pale, and brown faces looking forward, gazing down, blowing their noses, wiping the corners of their eyes. They're a unified mass. There might as well be only one person there, with their name being Many.

Someone dry heaves just outside the door to the little hall leading to the rectory. Dad is bent over, his body disappearing behind the wall but visible from the waist down. Only he would wear gardening shoes with his suit. Hopefully there is a trashcan there or at least a potted plant, but if not, I'm sure it's not the first time this place has cleaned up a little vomit. His attempt to purge is its own type of dirge. He's literally trying to expel his grief.

But those flowers...

I've never seen flowers like that. So, so many. How many petals there are? Tens of thousands, for sure. From where I sit, they sparkle—the convergence of the overhead lights and the fact I've not slept since it happened. They're like a beacon, like they're meant to be so beautiful, maybe it will tempt Tommy back to his body.

Almost hypnotized, I rise and shuffle out of my seat. The aisle from a front pew to an altar is something you take in baby steps, no matter the occasion, but now it's almost like a form of resistance. I don't want to stand beside that casket, so I ascend the altar steps at an angle.

At the corner of the platform, a huge wreath rests on a stand with Tommy's school photo. He smiles crookedly, and his hair hangs over his forehead—the look he always thought was cool.

For a moment, all I can see are those beautiful petals. I reach out to pluck one of the chrysanthemums. It's disrespectful. Those are meant for Tommy. Their collective glory is meant to honor him.

*****

Do I take one of the chrysanthemums and put it in my pocket?
Make note of your choice!

Yes. Turn to page 3.
No. Turn to page 3.

"Little son of a bitch," someone whispers in one of the front rows.

"Now, now, he's just a kid himself," comes the response.

I shake my head. My temples are pounding. I draw a deep breath, then let it go.

I step toward the casket, my first time near a dead body, and press my hand over the lid where I presume Tommy's head to be. His blame practically radiates through the coffin at me, and I try to project my guilt right back at it, as if they can somehow cancel each other out. As if there is a world where guilt could ever overcome fault.

"*Kid* nothing. It's his fault, no matter what age he is."

I don't need to look back to know they are looking right at the back of my head. Everyone in the chapel must be doing the same. Like my head is covered in red x's and they're dripping with Tommy's blood.

I force my eyes onto the coffin. The casket is the "Olympia Bronze" model with a velvet interior. The stuffy sales director ran the specs in a faux-sympathetic European accent, convincing my parents that, since the service would need to be closed casket, they would be doing their little boy right to kick up for one of the more expensive models.

"We do have Daniel's college fund," Dad had said.

"We couldn't..." Mom had trailed off. She was asking "Could we?" with her eyes.

I'm not going to say it didn't hurt for them to use my future for that, but at the same time, it *is* my fault Tommy is dead. Because I was the one who was supposed to be watching him.

I'd been blowing away a bunch of loud-mouthed tweens in *WWII Online*, completely absorbed, when he popped into the living room doorway. It's like the world stops existing. Or like I cease to exist.

"I'm gonna swim for a bit," seems like such strange last words to me.

Should I have thought more about it? Sure. But he had been swimming by himself hundreds of times. He was fourteen, after

all, and a good swimmer. Better than me. He would swim and
then lie out on the deck chairs to dry. You don't drown in
daylight, damn it. At least, not until you do.

Mom found him. I was still on the couch.

"The right ones never die," someone says behind me from a
couple of rows back.

It was Tommy's girlfriend. When she showed up at the
funeral home, I was out front.

"Greet people," Dad had ordered while he walked Mom in.

All my "Hello, thanks for coming" tumbled from my lips like
static, and I couldn't meet anyone's eyes. When Tommy's
girlfriend approached, she was holding a soda from Sonic, and
she attempted to slosh it onto me. I guess her grip on the cup
squeezed the lid off at the wrong time, but the ice and Dr. Pepper
just seemed to sort of belch out, running down her hand and
wrist.

"That's right. You heard me, you piece of shit," she says
behind me.

Something lightly hits my hair and clatters between the
pews, out of sight. No doubt, she threw something at the back of
my head. It doesn't hurt, but my fists clench, and my vision
tunnels and flashes. I spin and open my mouth. The words
"Leave me the fuck alone" bubble at my lips.

I clamp my teeth shut so hard, the *clack* echoes in the hollow
of the altar.

At the far end of the chapel stands a shadow.

Not a figure cloaked in darkness. It is a person *made* of
shadow. Everyone's eyes are fixed directly on me, so no one is
seeing the same thing I do.

It's not *just* a person made of shadow.

It is Tommy.

I don't know how I know it, but I do. His features aren't easy
to make out, but it's like I know his essence is there. With a swing
of his hand, he beckons me forward, and then he disappears out

of sight. A murmur erupts throughout the crowd when I run straight down the altar steps and out the aisle.

It occurs to me I could be hallucinating. Maybe I've had some sort of psychotic break. It's crazy to run out of the chapel during my brother's funeral, chasing after his shadow.

I don't care. It's also such a relief to be getting the hell out of everyone's damning gaze.

At the vestibule, I turn toward a narrow hallway that makes a hard right. Around the bend is a pair of unisex bathrooms and a third door, which is closing even while I turn the corner. On it, a sign reads: "Showroom."

I storm through and step into a long room with coffins displayed down both walls. A door stands at the far end. The walls are wood paneled halfway from the floor—lush wood made of deep reds and blacks. The walls above are white. Hung between the coffins are paintings of white flowers.

In the middle stand three raised displays, each of which holds one of the higher-end coffins. I recognize the room, of course, as the one where my parents spent my college fund. The coffin front and center is the same model they spent it on. Tommy's shadow stands beside that one.

I still can't make out any of his actual features. In a way, it's like a drawing of Tommy someone carefully covered over in black Sharpie. Maybe I'm hallucinating, but it's not some trick of the light or me making something out of nothing. I'm seeing a full-blown figure whose every feature is pitch-black. Guilt claws up the back of my throat, along with some bile. My heart thuds in my chest like it is a sledgehammer.

"Tommy?" I try to say, but it comes out as a broken rasp. A bubble of snot wells from one of my nostrils when I say it. The tears I clenched up earlier well out now in a hot stream down my cheeks.

"I don't have time to explain," his shadow says, in a distant version of Tommy's voice. "But I'm in a bad place, and you're the only one who can help."

"Anything," I say. "What do you need me to do?"
Tommy points to the coffin.
"Get in."

*****

My brother needs me. I'm getting in. Turn to page 160.

In a coffin? Hell no. Turn to page .7

This doesn't seem right. After all, my least favorite movie trope is "I don't have time to explain." There's *never* a case where a few words wouldn't clean everything up for audience and characters alike.

If this is somehow Tommy's ghost, is ghost business that much more complicated? If it's all in my head, will I climb into the coffin, only to find a security guard dragging me out a few minutes later, with an even more devastated version of Mom and Dad looking on? I can hear them now, while I get marched down the chapel aisle in handcuffs, my eyes all red from pepper spray.

Haven't you done enough? they'd say. *You already destroyed our family; you have to humiliate us now too?*

I look at the shadow of my brother right where his eyes should be. The divots of his sockets, a peak that is his nose...He doesn't seem to reflect light. It's rather like the light just stops at his skin.

The longer I look, the more guilt slithers about in my belly and under my skin. A deep sadness wells up in my chest, like my heart is alone in a freezer. Fear churns up beneath it, and my breathing accelerates.

Tommy looks from me to the casket. Without being able to make out his eyes or discern the shape of his lips, how am I supposed to understand his intentions? My guts are torn between telling me to run and to fall over and die.

The casket itself is lined with lush velvet which lusters in the light. The indented buttons capture just enough shadow to bring out the contoured fibers. The exterior varnish is streaked with the reflection of the overheads, and the whole display throws a shadow of itself onto the floor.

I shake my head and take a step back. If this is Tommy, it is not a version of him I should be interacting with.

Tommy's head dips as if with regret. A rattling sigh escapes him. He steps onto the shadow of the coffin and looks at me again.

I shake my head. What else am I supposed to do? I can't just go climbing into showroom coffins every time I hallucinate the brother who died because of me.

Tommy nods slightly. He lowers himself, sliding forward on the shadow, as if he is climbing into a coffin of his own. His whole form vanishes into the two-dimensional shape on the floor until only his arm is visible. That arm reaches up, grasps the shadow of the lid, and jerks it shut.

It closes with a loud thump, making me leap straight into the air with a yelp. When my feet hit the ground, I stumble and take a step back to steady myself.

I bump into something solid.

Somewhat soft.

Living.

Before I can react, something whisks down over my face. It hooks under my chin and jerks against my windpipe. The air cuts off, and my fingers climb, finding a cord of some kind. My mouth opens in a futile gasp, but no air comes through. My feet kick against the floor, but whatever is tightening that cord is stronger than I've ever hoped to be. It's like thrashing against steel.

"Guess this will have to do," something whispers in my ear.

My vision goes black, and a droning sound fills my ears.

***

The correct answer was to get inside the coffin.

Turn to page 160.

"I'm taking a lot on faith here." But I grab Shadow Tommy's hand and let him pull me upright.

When my leg is over the coffin's side, he steadies me, and I hop out. I land on the display platform and step to the mound of rock it stands upon. Together, Shadow Tommy and I slide to the level of the quartz urchins. It's still cold down here, but the wind doesn't whip through like above. Nonetheless, something inside my chest feels utterly frozen. Each beat of my heart sends a chill through my whole body.

Shadow Tommy shuffles toward the spiny stones. Now that I stand among them, they're even larger than they originally seemed and taller than I am. Despite that, Shadow Tommy pulls my arm until we're both crouched. He points to a narrow path between the spines.

I can make out his face even better now. It's almost like the way eyes adjust to a dark room. Though it's still nearly black, Tommy's features are more defined, and they're fraught with worry.

The path ahead is narrow, hardly a foot wide. In some places, the needle spikes of the quartz urchins practically interlock.

"Whatever you do, don't touch the spines," Shadow Tommy says.

"Why not?"

He rolls his eyes. For the first time, it strikes me that what would normally be the whites of his sclera are pure black, but his irises are a deep, lustrous purple.

"If all you do is touch them, they'll still snag...your shadow, and you'll tear pieces of...it away before you even know what you're doing. And if they break your skin, their poison will be in your blood before you can so much as blink."

"Poison?" I ask.

Shadow Tommy grabs my wrist and jerks me forward.

"We have to move."

"But I don't want to go through there," I say.

His grip is powerful, and his pull is incessant. My feet follow him for the sole reason that, if I resist, I'm certain he'll pull me over. I don't want to fall in a place surrounded by poisonous spines.

Nonetheless, I also become aware the ground beneath me is vibrating like a long peal of distant thunder, shaking everything. The quartz urchins seem to shiver too, their spines quivering like plucked strands in a spider's web. A little puff of white dust bursts from some of their tips.

"Run," Shadow Tommy hisses.

He takes off between the urchins, turning sideways and ducking his head forward and back to avoid the spines. The clearance beneath them seems the largest near their bases, so I drop into a crawl and scuttle close to the earth, keeping my head low, trying to twist my neck around as much as possible to make sure I'm not about to scrape my scalp. The shaking intensifies beneath me, and I chance a glance over my shoulder when I'm past the first two urchins.

The rise upon which the coffin's platform rested shudders violently and bursts into a shower of stone. A pitch-black head bludgeons up through it, shattering the coffin into pieces between massive jaws. The shadow beast strikes me as some sort of moray eel. A huge bulbous eye looks straight toward me from the side of its head.

With a high-pitch hiss like a squealing fan belt, it whips its head about, flinging pieces of the coffin and stone in all directions. They arc overhead, some crashing around me, others sailing far off. The ones striking the urchins shatter many of the spines. Sharp shards and even whole lengths streak like arrows. A massive spike embeds itself in the ground hardly six inches from my leg.

Hands thrust under my armpits. I'm being dragged backward.

"Are you crazy?" Shadow Tommy shouts in my ear. "It sees us!"

For a moment, I'm still hypnotized by the beast. It cocks its head toward me, even as two huge appendages drive upward. The massive arms—initially pressed to its side so tightly they were nearly invisible—unfurl and spread. Huge flesh flaps fall out and snap taut when its joints fully extend.

Wings. That damn thing has wings.

"Run," Shadow Tommy bellows. He lets go of me and breaks into an agile sprint, weaving the narrow path ahead.

The spell of the creature breaks, and I take off after Tommy's shadow, trying to stay on my feet. I brush against one of the spines, and its sharp tip slides through the fabric of my jacket. It cuts through the outer layer, but it only snags a bit on my button-down shirt.

A line of utter cold runs through my body down into my leg, and it's like it pulls out of me when I move. A black thread runs from my back to the spine I brushed, and a profound sadness floods me. I want to collapse to the ground, but instead, I reach up and brush my hand through the shadow thread. It immediately dissipates. The oppressive feeling abates enough, I remember I need to be running.

Ahead, Shadow Tommy has entered what looks to be a small clearing, or at least a space with a little elbow room. He stops and looks back, waving me forward frantically with his arms. Something churns behind me—a sound of things falling and grinding. I don't need to see it to know the winged eel has launched, and I half expect its shadow to glide over me, like it is some massive hawk. Though, since it seemed to be shadow itself...

I duck under one last spike and look up. Shadow Tommy grabs a hold of me by the shoulders and points. I follow his arm to the mouth of some sort of cave vanishing into the ground at a forty-five-degree angle. A pale, viscous slime drips from jagged outcroppings in the ceiling. It smells like rotten eggs, and a yellowish vapor seems to rise from the trails flowing down the cave's decline. My eyes burn, and so does the inside of my nose and mouth when it reaches me.

"Get in!" Shadow Tommy yells. Behind him runs a broad avenue through the quartz urchins that I could bolt through in a full sprint.

Just then, a great flapping comes from above. The winged eel soars high into the sky and tucks its wings back to its side. Its long body arcs downward. I already know: It's going to plunge straight at me like a diving hawk.

Beside me juts a massive urchin spine. It's at least ten feet long, the longest I've seen so far. If I brace it against rocks closest to me, it would be like a medieval spear against a cavalry charge.

Shadow Tommy dives into the cave.

*****

If it can come out of the ground, it can go into it. I'm going to run for it. Turn to page 18.

I follow Shadow Tommy. He knows this place better than me. Turn to page 13.

I'm going to embrace my inner pikeman and skewer that thing on the urchin spike. Turn to page 140.

I hold my breath and throw myself headfirst into the rank hole. The stench overwhelms me instantly, and the acrid fumes make my skin tingle. The viscous goo is thick as Vaseline, and it clings to my body in stretchy strands, like a hawked loogie.

For half a second, I believe Shadow Tommy must have duped me into diving into the goo…

But he's crowding beside me. The massive darkness blocks out almost all the light before swooping back into the air with a screech. I creep to the mouth of the tunnel and peer up. The beast arcs overhead again, and with steady flaps of its massive wings, it hovers above the hole.

Shadow Tommy shakes some of the ooze from his hands, pulling it apart like taffy. "That was close, but we're safe here."

"Why didn't it dive right in?" I ask.

"The smell. It can hold its breath for hours at a time while it tunnels, but when it surfaces to hunt, it breathes deep."

"But what is it?"

"It"—Shadow Tommy points at the sky—"is a winged shadow eel."

"Eels live in the ocean."

"And this was an ocean." A huge globule of goo drips from the cave ceiling onto Shadow Tommy's shoulder. "We're on the edge of what's now called the Boiled Sea. It was once called the Twilight Sea, but—"

"It boiled?" I ask. "So those spiky things really *are* sea urchins?

The shadow nods.

"The Shadowlands is old as time itself, maybe even older, and for lack of a better way to put it, it's the place where shadows live and have always lived."

"So, they don't live on the ground by our feet?"

"The shadow you see in the World of Light is just a reflection of your shadow's being, projected into this world by the power of the light. The Shadowlands, too, was once a grand place, much like your world, with towering cities and a thriving landscape.

During that time, a being called The Eater of Light watched over the world and prevented the awful power of the sun from destroying its dim beauty.

"Unfortunately, a rogue cult everyone calls The Thirteen banished The Eater of Light, and without its protection, the world was destroyed by the awesome violence of light in The Great Flare. The ancient kings and their kingdoms were brought to near instant ruin, and those that remain were subjugated among the ruins and forced to worship The Thirteen. Even now, they're worshipped as The Unlucky Number, and it is believed that if you don't pray to them, horrible misfortune will befall."

I scratch the back of my head.

"Okay, that's all fabulous, but what am I doing here? Why are *you* here? Are you Tommy?"

Shadow Tommy looks down and runs his hands through his hair. It's strange because they almost seem to disappear when he does so. I lose track of where his fingers end and the hair begins.

"So, as you might guess, not just anyone from the World of Light can enter The Shadowlands, and even the ones who can can't come and go as they please," Shadow Tommy says. "Otherwise, everyone would know about it."

"Oh yeah. I'd be first in line to get eaten by a flying eel while weaving my way through a field of poisonous gigantic sea urchins in what used to be an ocean."

"We might have entered The Shadowlands a bit off the beaten path. But I'll get to that in a moment. The thing is, Light is damaging here. If you are what we call a Brilliant person—someone happy and full of hope—you'd bring that Light here and be like a miniature sun."

"I'd boil the sea?"

"Not quite that. You could cause problems. So, the people who enter need to have heavy shadows, and one thing that increases the weight of your shadow is to have darkness helping to pull you across. Even with the shadowless, it's the apathy that pulls them through."

"The shadowless?"

"Sound out the words, dude," Shadow Tommy says. "Folks without shadows. Without darkness, no ambition. Without fear, you got no fight. They show up here time to time, all lost and aimless, and they tend to vanish in the darker places."

I wipe some of the stinking goo from my chest and shake it off my fingers.

"I can come here because I feel so guilty about Tommy, isn't it?"

"That's part of it…" Shadow Tommy trails off.

"And the other part?"

"Some people…The Shadowlands has business with them."

I slump back against the wall of the tiny cave. It's like reclining into reeking Jell-o, but I don't care. Everything has been unreal since Tommy drowned. Hell, I've always been a bit spaced, always ready to zone out to a game or a show binge, but this…This is different. I don't know exactly what it means to have business in The Shadowlands, but it is quite clear: I don't want to.

"How can this place have business with me? I didn't even know it existed."

"Well, you know how Tommy had been badly bullied a couple years ago?" Shadow Tommy asks. "Then how things got better?"

"Of course I know. Some of the only memories I'm truly proud of are when I helped him."

Mom and Dad knew too, especially after the day he came home with the black eye, a swollen lip, and a notice of suspension. Apparently, he decided to stand up for himself and belted the other kid across the face with a math book. The bully tackled him and punched him in the face, and they were both suspended as part of the school's zero tolerance policy.

Up until then, the bullying had grown increasingly relentless, which was what caused Tommy to lash out, but it didn't matter to the administration. Our parents went on about it for weeks, even getting on the news. It wasn't long after that things turned around for Tommy and he became really popular. Being on the news gave him enough celebrity for the 180.

"Well, things didn't get better for Tommy for the reasons you think," Shadow Tommy says. "The day he was suspended, he was so filled with darkness that he found his way into The Shadowlands on his own, and he made a deal with an agent of one of the most powerful beings in this whole place. A Shadow Broker named The Shadower."

"Shadow Brokers?"

"They trade shadows and parts of shadows for favors. Things that involve the nature of your shadow. For example, you might consider trading part of your shadow to forget your guilt over what happened to Tommy. In Tommy's case, he wanted to be popular. Respected. And The Shadower has ways of making that happen. The trick is that you have to pay him back within a certain amount of time before he gets to keep the shadow you gave him."

"Does that mean he traded you?"

This time, it is Shadow Tommy who winces.

"It would be more accurate to say he *indentured* me. But yes, he used me to make a deal, and you letting him drown prevented him from paying back his end of the deal."

I may not know much about The Shadowlands, but that can't be a good thing.

"What do I need to do?" I ask.

"You need to finish what Tommy started, or I'm going to belong to The Shadower, and your shadow will be lost to The Shadowlands forever."

*****

Doesn't seem like I have much of a choice now, do I? Tell me what to do. Turn to page 25.

No. I don't think working for this Shadower is going to make anything better. Turn to page 29.

Two things I know for sure: First, I'm sick of this place already, and second, I'm not diving into a slimy hole to escape something that clearly has no problem coming in and out of the ground. I shove Shadow Tommy aside and bolt past him down the wide avenue through the urchins. It's not as broad as something like an alley, but I don't need to duck and bend to get through unscathed.

A sickening crack like something shattering rings behind me.

Did the beast just take Shadow Tommy?

My feet kick up broken shards and pebbles. Rock crashes into stone, and heavy things fall unseen while I blaze forward. The wind of the eel creature wooshes over me when it swoops back up from its dive and soars over the spiny maze. Can it still see me? I can't see it. The black urchins are just barely too tall, and their spikes mean that, even if I stopped, I couldn't try to get an angle to view much more than straight up.

I keep expecting the creature's shadow to fall across me, but it is shadow itself, so it casts none. Plus, if I take my eyes off the path, it would be too easy to run straight into one of the black spikes.

Instead, I charge on, even as something I can only describe as a strange energy gathers in the air. I leap before the shadow creature crashes into the ground right through the space I just occupied. Shards of whatever the ground is made of smack against my shoulders and sting the back of my neck. The blows send me staggering forward, my arms pinwheeling, but I manage to keep my footing.

I suck in a deep breath against burning ribs. Though I'm young, I'm no runner. Ahead, the path forks, and for a moment, I hope somehow, if I take the correct turn, I'll get to better cover. Unfortunately, the beast bursts from the ground, apparently having dived straight under. It blocks the path to the right. I pivot to the left, but again, I'm no distance athlete.

I put a little too much weight on my ankle at an awkward angle. White light fills my head and bone cracks, like a branch collapsing off a tree trunk in the woods. I pitch sideways. An image of myself impaled on the urchins' spikes flashes into my mind, but I crash low enough to slide beneath them. The jagged ground rips through my clothes and into my flesh, like I'm sliding across a cheese grater covered in knives. My heart beats, and blood rushes out of my body in a hundred different spots. The bones of my lower leg stick out and down, just over the mouth of my shoe.

I suck a deep breath and shriek with every fiber of my being. The force of doing so sends a fresh thunderclap of pain exploding from my destroyed foot. My back spasms, and I thrash my hips to the side, but my only reward is yet another agonizing blast.

My voice breaks like a dropped vase, and air streams from my lungs in a shrill whistle. My vision is a field of dead black static popping with white sizzles. My nerves fire in panic, but my eyes manage to process fuzzy splotches. Sweat pours down my face. I lock my leg joints as strongly as my muscles can manage and allow my lungs to suck down air.

An object before me tucks into a spiny wreath of the urchin quills. A fractured oval. Its two halves tilt away from each other. It is massive. Big as me. From it leans a smaller version of the pitch-black beast I've been fleeing. Stones tumble and urchin spines snap in the path behind me, and the smaller creature lets out a high-pitch whine. The big one responds in a deep, sonorous rumble.

The creature lunges out of the egg and drives its jaws straight into my belly. The agony returns, tearing its way through the flesh and sinew. Blood bursts from my mouth, and finally, a single terrific thrust shoves its snout into my rib cage. Bones shatter when its tongue forces between its teeth and rips out my heart.

***

You did not make the correct choice. Try again.
Turn to page 12.

Make note of this choice at the front of the book or on a scrap paper with your other choices.

The morning sun glints on the zipper running right up to Miela's throat. I hesitate, unable to let myself forget she is unnatural, no matter how human she looks otherwise. It is like watching one of those movies where a character turns out to be a robot in disguise. To my eye now, she is totally human, but I can't stop picturing her unzipped, remembering that void with the scales. I don't know what else is in there, but more importantly, I don't know if there *is* anything else different about her. It's just as possible she'll unscrew her head to reveal a fully automatic turret built into her neck.

Nonetheless, I lean over the cart edge. The ground appears clear of the shadow scorpions that brought the man down, but I don't know where they came from to begin with. Do they live underground? Are there signs I should watch for? What other predators and dangers might live out here?

"It's okay, kid," the man rasps. "I've got this."

I eye him skeptically, and after a moment, I reach forward and pull his pant leg a couple of inches up his calf. Several sites where the stingers struck him above his shoes are massively puffy and purple, oozing a cloudy fluid from pock marks at their centers.

"They hurt," the man says, "but I'll manage."

The dryness in his voice reminds me of just how thirsty I am. My stomach rumbles too. I turn to Miela, hoping my eyes are wearing their most imploring look.

"This is insane," I say. "He needs to rest. He needs food and water."

Miela scoffs.

"He's not getting food and water," she says.

"That will kill him."

Miela tugs at the hem of her shirt and sits upright. The zipper wobbles in the light, and a knot forms in my stomach.

"And once again, you know so damn little and think you know everything. He will pull this cart without his name. Without food or drink. Until he collapses and dies. Then, he will return to the World of Light, recover his strength, come back here, and do it again."

"Wait," I say. "Dying here sends him back to the World of Light? So if I—"

Miela shakes her head firmly.

"Usually, casters cannot die in The Shadowlands. We're meant to be a flicker here, a brief visitor, never welcome but tolerated because we bring things The Shadowlands desires. That The Shadower desires. You...You are here for more complicated purposes than a barter of batteries or umbrellas."

"And those purposes are...?"

Miela says nothing.

Well, that's lovely. For a moment, I had found my ticket home. Is there even a way for me to get home? What if I'm *that* different? What if they plan to hollow me out and install me with my very own torso zipper and scale?

The man sits up in the cart beside me. His hand closes over my shoulder. It is knobby, and there is a coolness to his grip. It's like he just walked out of a freezer.

"It really is okay, kid." The man reaches down to his legs and lifts them over the side of the cart. He heaves his butt onto the edge and drops to the obsidian road. His face twists with the pain of the impact, but he grits his teeth and walks to the front of the cart, stepping over the nearest pole. He then spits in his hands, wets his palms, and takes up his burden.

"Once you understand The Shadowlands, it looks very different," Miela says.

"My teachers said that about pre-calculus, and even after I figured it out, I still hated it."

Miela rolls her eyes, but she reaches underneath the seat. When she pulls a canteen out, I hold out my palm to stop her.

With a laugh, she says, "It's real water. It'll taste like shit because everything starts to taste like shit here, but it'll keep you going."

I take the canteen. Miela doesn't let go.

"I know what you're thinking," she says. "Don't offer it to him. He'll say no, but all he'll think about is what if he'd said yes. Just because he'll be alive and well in the World of Light doesn't mean dying of thirst here isn't horrible."

"*Being* here is horrible," I reply.

We ride in silence for a while after that. The man pulls us up a gradual incline which takes us into a field of stones of varying and increasing size. We wind in long arcs among them. The slope climbs so slow, I hardly notice until the man starts to grunt when he plants his feet. We get deeper into what seems to be some kind of foothills, with a huge, snowcapped mountain range ahead on the horizon. The road splits around some sort of large rock formation and converges on the other side.

Down one branch of the fork, the obsidian road is broken and jagged.

Down the other, two figures are huddled. One of them appears to be lying prone while the other hunches over them, shaking them perhaps. It's hard to say from here because they're shadows and the lack of ease to see lines makes their size hard to read, but I'm pretty sure they're children.

The upright kid looks back over its shoulder, but I'm too far away to make out any other features.

"Hey!" the kid says, jumping up and waving their arms. "Hey! Come quick! She fell!"

Miela mouths the word *no* at me.

Are they kidding, or what?

I climb out of the cart and take a few steps toward them.

*****

They're kids and they need help. Turn to page 87.

You can't trust anything here. Take the broken road.
Turn to page 82.

"I'm sorry I don't have a better deal for you, but good deals are hard to come by here," Shadow Tommy says as I grunt my assent. He places his hand on my back and nudges me towards the mouth of the tunnel.

I resist, not wanting to become monster food.

"What is it I'm supposed to do?" I ask.

"I just need you to find someone and get him to follow you to a hearing with The Judge. The fella's a big problem, mind you. Done some damage to things way bigger than himself."

"Okay...a judge...That doesn't sound too bad." And it actually doesn't. If there are judges, then there is civilization. This place might be more than just death-trap urchin mazes.

"Not 'a judge', The Judge. And it's going to be a bit tougher than it sounds because the person you're finding knows he's going to be in trouble. But I think that someone with a story like yours might get him to listen. But we can deal with the difficulties when we're almost there. The good news is that, as long as we're coated in this goo, the shadow eel will leave us alone."

I take a tentative step forward and look up. There is no sign of the flying shadow anywhere.

Nonetheless, I say, "I think maybe it would be better if I just died in here."

A strange look flashes across Shadow Tommy's face, but then he looks back into the tunnel and fouls his nose. He shakes his head.

"You made a deal; you need to keep it," he says. "Besides, we came into The Shadowlands just on the edge of the Boiled Sea. It's not far to the border."

"Why couldn't we have come some place friendlier?"

"Because when the Cult of The Thirteen took over, they made a lot of laws against trying to help The Eater of the Light. See, The Thirteen were helped by people from the World of Light, and people from the World of Light always have and always will want to control things. If The Shadowlands returns to its former glory, they'd never be able to contain it."

"Yeah, that sounds like us." I picture a restaurant selling McShadow burgers under black arches on the edge of the parking lot of Wal-Dark-Mart. There isn't any doubt they would be drilling for oil in no time and mining for actual black gold.

"Anyways, we've got to move. We're safe from the eel, but there's other things out here we don't want noticing us."

Shadow Tommy darts into the urchin maze. He keeps low but moves quick enough, and following drives me too out of breath to ask questions. Though we take several turns along the way, we seem to move in the same direction underneath the smoldering coal in the sky.

My skin gets all goose-pebbly under my slime-damp clothes, and the cold bite of the wind begins to burn. Shadow Tommy doesn't seem to notice. His attention is focused on the turns and the sky. That is all fine and well. So far, nothing I would deem normal conversation has escaped from his mouth anyway.

But it does strike me that the urchins seem to be getting deeper around us. They are becoming interlaced with some other shadowy structure. It is a strange, lattice-like substance, almost crystalline in its appearance. The way it twists, bends, and holds faintly cratered contours is vaguely familiar. All deep shades of purple and blue and even what seems to be some sort of maroon, so dark it is almost black, shine and luster even in the dim light of the Shadowland sun.

Coral. It reminds me of coral.

And the path we are taking descends into it. The route ahead forms into a tunnel, not gooey like the one we hid from the shadow eel in, but brittle and sharp. The ground grows pitted, like it is coral itself. Like it will turn an ankle in a heartbeat. I've been through enough caves on field trips in my lifetime to know bad road when I see it.

"Is this safe?" I ask. "Like, shouldn't we go over it?"

Shadow Tommy chuckles. "Oh, sure. Just go your own way. What do I know about the place I've existed in for so much longer than you?"

Unfortunately, I do not see another route, and there are, by far, enough urchin spikes and other sharp outcroppings I don't fancy climbing over. Nonetheless, I look up at the huge hill of coral. How deep and vast was the sea to allow a reef this size to grow within it?

A sharp crack brings me back to the path. I can barely make Shadow Tommy out in the mouth of the tunnel, but it looks like he broke a bit of coral off the roof of the cave. With a casual toss, it arcs from his hand. I expect it to land on the ground with a clatter, but instead, it hits with a *plunk*.

Around it, a ring of soft aqua glow radiates and spreads down the tunnel. A liquid of some kind. Shadow Tommy breaks off another skinny outcropping and tosses it in. The glow intensifies and spreads further into the darkness, lighting the whole area. The cave itself isn't much different than any other, with some ribbony formations running all along it.

The stream, however...I've never seen anything quite like it. Its source appears to be the ground beside Shadow Tommy, and it falls sideways like a horizontal waterfall. The glow shines off droplets spraying up and away from the main flow, and turbulence swells wherever the stream breaks over rock outcroppings. It reminds me of the bioluminescent bays in Puerto Rico I learned about on some nature documentary on Netflix or something.

"Woah," I whisper, creeping forward and reaching toward the source of the flow. I picture my fingers plunging in and that same glow intensifying around them.

"Just don't touch the water," Shadow Tommy says.

I jerk my hand back. When Shadow Tommy smirks at me, though, I roll my eyes.

*****

Touch it. How often am I going to see a sideways flowing, luminescent waterfall? Turn to page 31.

Sigh...I supposed I'd better not. Turn to page 33.

I study Shadow Tommy's face. In the poor light caused by the combination of the dim sun and the shelter of the tunnel, his edges are oddly blurred, much the way his hand blurred into his hair while we talked. His outline practically seems to ebb into the shadows around him. Were it not for the faint glistening of the mucus-like ooze, his boundaries might have failed altogether, pouring his being into the air around him.

I shake off the thought and try to read this weird echo of my brother's expression, locking my gaze with his. Beneath the uncanny darkness of his features, a strange uncertainty swims, and my gut urges me to get away.

This whole thing sounds way too much like deals with the devil combined with some sort of bizarre human trafficking. Even if I was in some way responsible for Tommy drowning, I can't imagine that taking part in this is going to make anything better for anyone in a way that isn't awful.

"Look, man," I say. "I think I'd rather do what I can to make this up to my parents. Or, maybe not make it up, but at least get them to forgive me. Or be okay with living with what happened. When things like this happen, there's ways we're supposed to move forward with our lives."

"You think your parents will ever forgive you?" he asks with a sneer. "You're the lazy thing that's always occupying the couch. The thing who couldn't do one simple job. Tommy was popular with them too. The 'height of popularity' is the expression, really. If they abide you to continue to live with them, they'll never let you forget that you destroyed their family."

Every single word is a dagger in my heart, opening something cold inside, like a frozen wound that widens and widens. Tears force themselves from my eyes with an ugly sob that sends snot bubbling from my nostrils.

"I've had it," I snap. "I followed you because I thought that maybe Tommy had a message or something. Or, hell, maybe that I'd just gone crazy. But this..." I gesture to the tunnel and the mucus, and then I turn and wave my hands at the urchins and whatever the hell waits outside. "This is too much."

Something squelches by my feet, and I spin back to find Shadow Tommy crouched and grabbing something out of the muck. As he rises, my eyes fall to his hand. He's holding a broken urchin spine.

I open my mouth to ask "What are you doing" as I try to take a step back, but his other hand shoots up and closes around my throat. His face is wrought with agony and desperation, his every feature trembling, his eyes so wide I see the whole purple iris and the black space all around.

"If you'd been willing, we both would have had a chance," he says.

With a lightning swing of his arm, he rams the urchin spine down my throat. It's long enough to bludgeon its way deep into my torso even as my teeth shatter and my jaw snaps. The pain is like nothing I've ever felt, and my body spasms with an urge to run away from itself in all directions at once. The spine's tip must have some sort of opening because as the object rips its way further down, the convulsions of my body send blood and bile spurting up and out of the conical hollow.

The world fades to darkness and a burbling static. I'm barely aware that Shadow Tommy begins to pour himself down the tube into me, like it's some sort of shadow funnel.

***

You chose wrong. The correct answer was Doesn't seem like I have much of a choice now, do I? Tell me what to do.
Turn to page 25.

Without another word, I step forward and stick my left hand straight into the surreal flow. The force of the stream is surprisingly strong, and my whole arm struggles to hold my palm against it. The water lights while sluicing around my fingers, palm, and wrist, and my eyes fill with the gem-like brilliance. I smile and laugh despite just how cold the liquid really is.

It's so frigid, in fact, the water striking my arm has frozen solid. There's a cuff around my wrist, and flows of ice snake through the stream like lightning bolts. It's like those TikTok videos where someone flash freezes a bottle of water by shaking it.

I try to jerk my arm free, but the ice has spread, like a casing around the whole source of the stream. It's rapidly extending down the tunnel.

"It's gonna bite me in the ass," Shadow Tommy says. "But holy shit, it's funny to see how dumb shadow casters can be."

The flesh of my wrist and forearm turns blue and white and gleams like mica in the luminescence. A lance of cold and pain starts in the center of my arm bones and crawls toward my shoulder. I jerk my arm again, but I'm totally unable to budge it. The way the pain creeps upward is like trying to swallow too large a mouthful of water.

I grab my elbow with my other hand, as if I can choke off the progress of the cold, but the skin at the joint burns my fingers like dry ice, even as they grip. Patches of skin tear off my fingertips.

I bellow and thrash against the titanic hold the waterfall has on me, planting my feet and throwing my weight back. White-hot agony sears in my shoulder when the joint dislocates, but my hand is still fixed.

I thrust my free hand toward Shadow Tommy, but he just waves.

"You know...I forget sometimes how much less resilient bodies from the World of Light are than us shadowfolk. A shame you won't just go home, like the rest of you casters."

The frozen thrust inside my arm reaches my shoulder. My heart thuds against my ribs like a caged animal. My eyes are so wide, they might fall out of my skull. Convulsions spasm through me, and my knees buckle. I lurch sideways, and my shoulder and chest plunge straight into the flow.

The glow flares around me, beautiful, like I'm being engulfed. Like some intangible, frozen angel. Something inside me crackles and grinds, and then, my chest locks up.

Blackness swarms my vision, and agony screams from my frozen heart.

***

You chose wrong. The correct answer was Sigh...I supposed I'd better not. Turn to page 33.

With a long sigh, I stick my hands in my pockets. My body writhes with a sense of disappointment. The feeling is strange. I really *want* to stick my hand into that water. It's like my eyes miss the glow, even though the water is still illuminated. I want it to be brighter. Closer. To cover my whole body and pour down my throat.

My god, I bet it tastes so good, like the perfect cold drink on a hot summer day. When I stare into it, it's like my eyes don't see anything else and my body vanishes around me.

"You feel it, don't you?" Shadow Tommy snaps off another bit of stone or coral—or whatever it is—and my body clenches when he lobs it into the flow.

When the glow flares, it's like my spine is a plucked guitar string and all my nerves go on end. My hands are out of my pockets before I realize it, but I jerk them back. It's physically painful to turn my head away from the water. My hands go clammy, and my heart hurtles against my ribs.

"What the hell is happening to me?"

"Just keep following me," he says. "And try not to look directly at the glow. It'll get worse before it gets better, but don't touch the water."

Shadow Tommy is careful to stay to the right side of the tunnel, brushing his fingers against the wall, so I do the same. The stone is cold and rough under my touch, but it's somehow reassuring, and it helps keep my mind from seeking out the light. I keep the rest of my focus on my feet, stepping around little pits and divots, some of which look deep enough to die in.

The glow in the water fades, and once again, Shadow Tommy throws something else into it. The pull is even more powerful this time. I literally imagine myself leaping straight into the light with arms outstretched, like I'm going to give it a great big bear hug.

"Stop doing that," I say through gritted teeth.

"We need light." Shadow Tommy shrugs, and he's not wrong. The pitted ground could turn an ankle or break a leg.

"It's getting worse," I say.

"Deal with it."

We press forward only as fast as the ground and the steadily dying light allow, but our progress is decent. Three more times, Shadow Tommy ignites the urge in me by setting off the luminescence. By the time I recover from the third, I'm weeping and trembling against cold sweat. I try not to vomit, but a bit of bile shoots into my sinuses before I manage to swallow it back down. It's like the worst flu I've ever suffered is kicking me in the nuts.

"I don't know if I can stand this." I lock my eyes on my shoes so I'm not tempted to glance at the light.

"Look," Shadow Tommy says.

I brace myself, clenching my fists so tight my fingernails bite into my palms. Slowly, I raise my chin. Shadow Tommy is pointing forward. I don't realize at first *where* he is pointing. There is no light in the water, but I can see him. I squint. There, some distance ahead, I make out the other end of the tunnel.

I can see my feet. Enough light is coming in, and I don't need the glow anymore.

Nonetheless, I look Shadow Tommy square in the face. "Can you toss one more in? Just so I can see it one last time?"

Shadow Tommy shakes his head.

"Trust me, if you never saw that light again, you'd be better off. That's why, in a minute here, I'm afraid I'm going to have to blindfold you."

My eyes widen, and I snort out a huge laugh. It tapers into smaller giggles, which die out when it becomes clear Shadow Tommy isn't joking.

I point to the still-pitted ground. "Yeah, that's a big no."

"The tunnel brings us out at the far side of the reef. This water flow is one of many that feed into the Sideways Lake border of the 'civilized' Shadowlands. As the separate waterflows collide with each other, they're *always* glowing. You'd never survive it."

"What is a Sideways Lake?"

"Well..." Shadow Tommy hesitates. "The physics of The Shadowlands doesn't always work the way it does in your world—"

"Like the fact that you're a three-dimensional talking shadow?"

"...Yeah, and that in some cases, a lake's surfaces might be vertical, with the water flowing upward into the sky."

"I'm calling bullshit. I'm going to have to see this."

Shadow Tommy lets out a long breath, and his shoulders slump.

"You're not the only way I can complete your brother's deal," he says. "I can't babysit you every single step of the way because there are a whole lot of ways to die in The Shadowlands."

*****

Dude, you'd better take a photo for me or something.
Turn to page 43.

Damn straight. I want to see a vertical lake.
Turn to page 36.

A vertical lake is something I just have to see. My being nearly killed by a shadow eel and the death of my brother at his damn pool prove life is too short to pass up something which sounds so spectacular. No one will believe me if I tell them what I have seen here, so if this trip is going to have any value, it's got to be for me.

No doubt, Shadow Tommy is worried I won't be able to resist the pull of the glowing water. The thought both scares and thrills me, but the fact is, now that I've seen it, I know what to expect. I don't know what will happen if I touch it, but I can resist it. The euphoria of the glow is powerful, but I've got free will.

Nonetheless, clamminess swaths my body. My hands, my armpits, the small of my back—I'm cool as fresh sushi. No way waiting is going to help. Just like with Band-aids.

"Let's do this," I say.

Shadow Tommy's face drops, and despite the darkness of his eyes, he's looking down and to the side. We're not going to get very far together if he doesn't have any faith in me, so this is going to prove I have what it takes to make it here.

With a wave of his arm, he turns and proceeds forward.

The change of the light is subtle at first, partially because I'm still focused on my feet far more than I am on what lies ahead. The first thing I notice is something new in the churn of the water flow—a different pitch of rumble. This one is far deeper and resonant in a way which creeps straight into my bones. It must be incredibly loud for me to hear it over the stream because the stream itself is deafening enough.

The way the edges of things, even in the shadows, start to shimmer catches me next. It's like the rocks around me are crawling with threads of color, and I raise my eyes. For the first time, I discern the way the water flow curves upward at the cave mouth, like a sheet hanging across the view of what lies beyond.

The pathway must descend from the opening, but from where I creep forward, it looks like nothing but open air. I pick up the pace because I'm so close to the tunnel's end, and I'm tired of being surrounded by stone. What is ahead? I must breathe the mist.

Shadow Tommy stops right in the path, and he leans against the tunnel wall like he's tired. I push by him, and he calls out at me. It might be a complaint or a call to caution since the ground is still treacherous, but with the light growing around me, the footing is easy. I bound from solid space over holes, trenches, and outcroppings, remembering days playing the floor is lava and how good I was at playground parkour as a kid. It's just so easy to move. So freeing.

Ahead, the light blooms, like someone slid up a dimmer switch to maximum, and a glorious teal glow floods me. The euphoria is immediate, and it engulfs my whole body. Pleasure rolls down my torso and into my limbs in waves, and the boundary where my figure ends and the air begins becomes incredibly fuzzy. My being is expanding to be everything. *I* am everything. The feeling is so singular, so overwhelming.

My eyes fill with a placid ovoid disc spanning the sky, like a massive mirror covered in froth. The foam itself pulsates with the same glow coursing through my veins, entering my every thought. If I dive forward into the flow while it sweeps from the cave mouth, it'll carry me up to that floating lake, and I'll swim like I'm flying. Soar like I'm diving.

Oh my god, I could just dissipate into this perfect cloud of myself and feel this incredible pleasure for all eternity. My ears fill with the ringing of thousands of pure notes.

Then the light cuts off all at once to total blackness.

My body screams with agony at the theft of pure bliss. A howl rises in my chest but won't reach my mouth. I try to throw myself forward. Pain explodes around my throat, and I lurch with both my legs, but my head just won't move. Something is crushing against my neck from all sides, pressing against my face.

I gag and hack, grab at my throat, but my fingers hit some taut barrier preventing me from taking hold. My thoughts break, and everything starts to recede. Something might be dragging me, but I can't be sure of anything.

"When Icarus flew towards the sun..." something says to me. It seems like either a whisper or really loud but coming from miles away. "He left his shadow in the maze with the minotaur. After his dad buried his physical body and went on with his life, he remained among those passages, angry and bitter. He took it on himself to start taunting the minotaur for the cruelty of his time imprisoned. The minotaur, feral, savage, couldn't understand how something could dash along the ground in front of it but not be there when it threshed the air in that spot with its horns.

"Day after day, Icarus's shadow tormented the beast, driving it further and further out of its mind. It began to charge blindly at the walls, shaking the labyrinth to its very foundation. One day, a tremendous blow to the end wall of a dead end brought down a patch of the ceiling, revealing dazzling beams of sunlight. The light fell upon the minotaur and threw its shadow to the ground, whereupon Icarus's shadow promptly fell upon it before it could gain its bearings.

"He bound it hand and food, tying its wrists and ankles behind its back and to its neck. It choked and sputtered until it succumbed to its own strangling pulls and went limp. Icarus's shadow then delivered the minotaur's shadow to The Shadower, for Icarus had never known that his father, Daedalus, bought the magic that drove the wings he'd made with a shadow debt, and that debt was finally paid."

I don't know entirely what to make of the story. My head is far too cloudy to contemplate it. I'm being led forward on a slow, meandering path, and I can't hear the water anymore. Whatever is over my head is so dark, absolutely no light breaks through. I weep and mutter, wanting to see the light. Just one look at the lake. If I get that, Shadow Tommy can knock me unconscious if he wants.

If he hears me, he does not respond.

After what seems like an eternity, we come to a stop, and the hood slides up and over my head.

***

Make note of your choice and continue on to page 40.

The sky is a wall of what I can only understand as static from horizon to horizon. It's a strange, nebulous cloud, like the world glitched out, the way Netflix gets when the Wi-Fi isn't working right. If I stare at any one spot, my eyes attempt to discern shapes, but I can't make out the lake or even be sure there really is sky somewhere beyond there.

I'm at the end of the world in an old video game, back before they mastered rendering horizon lines. A cobblestone path runs from directly beneath my feet to that barrier and ends in a dark spot in the static. I can only presume it is the opening through which we passed.

My heels are slick on the shiny stones beneath my feet. The material, covered in smooth curves, looks familiar. It almost reminds me of a deep purple marble or something.

Shadow Tommy rustles beside me.

"Obsidian," he says. "It's the main building material in The Shadowlands. This is Black Rock Pass, one of the only roads that crosses the Barrier."

"What the hell am I looking at?" I make a broad gesture at the end of the world.

"One of two barriers that holds back The Eater of Light from The Shadowlands," Shadow Tommy says. "Put in place by The Unlucky Number before either you or I were a dream of the universe."

Shadow Tommy takes me by the elbow and turns me around. The paved road runs up a gentle slope. At the crest of a ridge perhaps a hundred yards ahead, a row of columns stands like some ancient stone fence. The columns are curiously geometrical in shape, and my mind dredges up a photo from my geology textbook, the class most of the other kids called Rocks for Jocks. I took it because it's really easy to zone in and out while still kind of keeping up. They must be basalt. Basalt, I remember, is volcanic rock, just like obsidian.

I grunt and am about to comment on it, when my eyes fall upon a glowing window among the stone, and I make out a cabin around it. A silhouette in the window watches us intently.

Not a silhouette, I suspect. A shadow.

"What is that?" I say.

"It's called Synoro. Think of it as a checkpoint," Shadow Tommy says. "They register every soul that crosses the Barrier. Let's go."

We start up the slope.

I think back to a trip my parents took us on to Quebec, when Tommy and I were kids, to visit some cousins. We crossed the Canadian border close to dinner time. Tommy and I were so tired and grumpy, and our parents told us both to keep our mouths shut because they didn't want to get hassled.

I've always been anxious about crossing borders as a result, especially since the Canadian border had dogs and folks with guns. Oddly, the single cabin feels more welcoming than the line of booths across the road where customs officers waited.

Shadow Tommy approaches a door at the back of the cabin, reaches for the knob, and pauses. He looks over his shoulder and whispers urgently, "By the way, under no circumstances should you tell them your real name."

He opens the door before I can respond. The door creaks on its hinges, and Shadow Tommy strains to pull it ajar. When it's open wide enough for him to slip through, he does, and without any other options, I follow.

Inside, the space is simple. The room is lit by flickering lanterns, and a counter bisects it. Across the main space from where I entered stands another door. On a stool on the far side of the counter sits a shadow. A tall desk with a little typewriter upon it sits near the counter, and on its other side stands a tall barrel, kind of like the old-school rain barrel my friend Barret's dad keeps in his backyard.

My eyes return to the shadow. It isn't quite like Shadow Tommy. When I first looked at him, his form was almost a uniform black, and I couldn't make out his details until my eyes got used to looking at him. This shadow's face *is* a uniform black, like a department store mannequin the color of pitch. There are no discernible features. The surface of its skin almost resembles liquid, and the reflections of the lanterns shine off it.

No mouth opens, but the bottom of its face ripples when it speaks, like a pond vibrating from sound waves. The voice is devoid of tone, with an odd grit to it, almost like a more natural version of someone speaking through one of those old vibrating voice boxes.

"Name?"

Shadow Tommy clears his throat. I glance back to him. He raises his eyebrows at me as if to say "Well, we talked about this."

I turn back to the faceless thing on the other side of the counter. It does not have discernible eyes, but its attention bores holes right through me.

"This is for official border records," the clerk-thing says. "False responses violate code 37-B-2A of Shadow Law and are punishable by pain of servitude."

Shadow Tommy nudges the back of my heel with his shoe.

*****

I'm just going to trust Shadow Tommy's advice.
Turn to page 47.

Yeah, that's a "no" on pain of servitude. I'll give my real name.
Turn to page 53.

My heart aches at the thought of the chance to see an entire lake of that glow. I yearn for it the way I might pine for a hard crush or the arrival of the perfect vacation. Sweat beads up under my arms and at the back of my neck, tickling my skin when it trickles over the fine hairs. The words to refuse the blindfold rise in my throat, which is exactly why I know I must agree to it.

"Dude," I say. "You'd better take a photo for me or something."

Shadow Tommy snorts.

"So, I know you folk from the World of Light are used to carrying phones and cameras everywhere you go, but does this..." Shadow Tommy raises his arms in a sweeping gesture. "Does this look like a place with good cell service and charging stations everywhere?"

I smirk and pull my phone from my pocket, shocked I haven't used it once since I arrived. Haven't even thought about it. How is that possible? Any other day, I would have thought about it every other minute. I haven't scrolled any feeds in hours. Normally, I would have seen those urchins and snapped a few pictures. Hell, I probably would have been killed by that eel while trying to film the stupid thing for TikTok.

Then again, being transported in a coffin to a harsh world, where everything around you is trying to kill you, does tend to rearrange your priorities a little. One thing for sure: Getting a couple of hours to shut my brain off and play a few matches online has fallen way down on my list.

Shadow Tommy reaches out and takes the phone from my hand. He turns it over a couple of times and tilts it side to side. Then, with a snap of his wrist, he flings it to the cave floor. The screen's cracking is audible, as is the subsequent crunch when he smashes his heel down onto it.

"Holy shit, man!" I shout.

I lunge forward to grab a hold of Shadow Tommy, but he steps back and takes both my wrists in his hands. His grip is iron, and he twists my arms outward. I cry out and stop fighting. He can break both my wrists at will.

"After the lake, we pass through a border checkpoint," he says. "If they find this, they will not let us through. You don't want to know the consequences if they think you're here to bring proof of The Shadowlands to the Light."

He lets go of my wrists, and I rub them gingerly. The joints ache where his thumbs pressed hard into the bone.

"I don't want to prove shit to anyone," I say. "But I've had enough of this. I'm going back to my coffin."

"No, you won't." There's a grave seriousness to Shadow Tommy's tone.

Even though I was fully resolved to take my chances with the shadow eel, I need to listen to what he says next.

He continues. "You made a deal to see Tommy's deal through. You don't break a deal in The Shadowlands. There are consequences."

"Oh yeah. Because that's so much worse than freaking everything about this place."

"A decade of hard labor," Shadow Tommy says. "You could end up—"

He hesitates when I open my mouth to rebuke him, but I close it again without saying anything. A decade of labor sounds bad enough, but it is clear ten years of work *here* probably means something even worse than it would in my world.

"Fine," I say. "Let's get this over with."

Shadow Tommy nods and pulls a strip of black cloth from his pocket. It doesn't surprise me he knew this was coming, but it does catch my interest. It means he has done this before. What should I read into that? However, when he reaches forward and wraps the cloth tightly around my eyes, I'm more struck by the way it smells—like dust and vinegar.

My feet shuffle hesitantly. He takes my elbow and leads me forward.

"If you let me fall into a hole, I'm going to make sure I drag you down with me," I say.

"That sounds like the spirit of The Shadowlands. You'll get comfortable here yet."

Our progress is slow and steady. The ground isn't too bad, but periodically, he gives me a stopping tug and instructs me to steer to one side or the other. At one point, we step two paces to the left, and tiny droplets of the glowing stream sprinkle against my arms. I draw in a deep breath, and my head gets all giddy.

The rumble of the stream has increased steadily in volume, and a great well of noise seems to lie ahead. In my mind's eye, I picture the glowing, frothy torrent. The way the water must splash and flow...up? Would it be so bad if I just pulled the blindfold down for one second?

The urge breaks off when Shadow Tommy's voice interrupts my thoughts. "We're almost to the mouth of the tunnel. You'll feel the space widen, and that's when the temptation will be the worst. Do *not* give into it. If you do, I fear I won't be able to stop you."

Even after he says it and falls quiet, the impulse resurges. I stick my hands into my pockets because they're literally itching to reach up and rip the cloth away. To make it worse, the glow I can't see is clearly intensifying. The slightest bit of its brilliance is penetrating through the black. It's like looking at a lightbulb with my eyes closed. Worms writhe under my skin. Something slithers beneath my scalp. I just *have* to know.

"Did you know that once a shadow called The Elder brought a blind woman through this tunnel, thinking he'd found a way to eliminate the temptation of the Light? The poor woman had been blind since birth. She didn't ever have eyes that worked; her sockets were empty things covered in flaps of useless flesh. At first, everything seemed to be going well. The Elder had triggered the water along the way to help guide them both. But as the light swelled when they neared the lake, the blind woman stopped.

She reached out with her hand and began to paw slowly at the air.

"The Elder asked her what was the matter, and she said she felt something incredible in the air, and it was making something happen in her mind she didn't understand. The Elder placed his hand on his chin and thought a moment, but he did not have any explanation.

"It was then that the woman raised her hands up to her empty eye sockets and shoved her fingers inside them. Gasping and sobbing as she did so, from within herself, she pulled out long ropes of shadow, and from those ropes spread fine filaments, like veins. They fell to the ground in a tangled heap, quivering, and an electric luster began to swarm over their surfaces. They began to bulge and rise, like bread in an oven, until they grew limbs and heads.

"When she was done, two completely formed figures stood before her, each with a single glowing eye in the center of its face, staring straight at her. She fell to her knees and wept, 'I can see myself!'

"Then, in unison, the two forms fell upon her, biting and clawing at her until one of them split her head open on the rocks."

Shadow Tommy stops and tugs me to a halt.

"Holy shit," I say. "What the hell is the moral of that?"

"No moral," Shadow Tommy says. "The Shadowlands are both amazing and awful."

His fingers brush at my temples, and he pulls the blindfold off my face.

***

Make note of your choice and continue on to page 40.

Something about the shadow-clerk's being fills me with anxiety. It's not just its inky facelessness; it's the way it looks at me without eyes, listens despite its ears being nothing more than a suggestion—only little lumps on the sides of its head. It does not have an expression, but somehow, it's frowning at me. Impatience radiates off it like heat.

It reaches up and lays both its palms onto the counter, its elbows slightly bowed outward. I don't want that thing knowing who I am, so I try to think of something I've been called before other than Daniel, Danny, or Dan.

The first things that pop to mind are the voices of my gaming buddies when I was fourteen. They gave me a particular nickname because I was obsessed with one of the original first-person shooter titles. The name always irritated me, but it is the only other name I can truthfully claim to be called.

"Doom Boy," I blurt.

Shadow Tommy snickers behind me, but the clerk-thing gives a slight nod. It reaches down and lifts a book onto the counter. I can't read the symbols on the cover. It opens the binding and flips forward. Dense script fills page after page, and I look around for a pen. There don't seem to be any "office" implements of any kind in sight. Finally, the shadow-clerk reaches a blank spot and turns the book toward me.

Am I supposed to write something? Should I have brought a pen?

The shadow-clerk's hands dart out with lightning precision and grab me by the shoulders. The thing pulls me forward with the unbreakable grip of a machine.

"Oh shit." My feet leave the ground.

Shadow Tommy calls out, "Hey now!"

Its face slides toward mine. My lower body bangs against the counter edge, and my torso leans forward across the barrier. It even smells like ink. An acrid stink floods my nostrils. I grab it by the wrists, but as much as it looks like liquid in its face, I might as well be gripping steel pincers. They yield nothing, no matter how hard I claw at them, and if I keep going, I'll rip my fingernails off.

The gap between us closes entirely, and its forehead presses against my temple. Its nose is next, and then its mouth. Its cheeks caress mine, impossibly close, pulling my face into its own. My vision blacks out when its eyes' divots cover my eyelids. It's like the world's most fucked-up kiss, and I'm not even on a first date.

My chest spasms because I suddenly want to gasp, but there's something adhesive about its contact, preventing any part of my face from moving. My throat makes little grunts, trying to exhale and suck back the bit of air I had in my lungs. I'm going to suffocate.

Its grip on my shoulders pushes away. My whole body moves in reverse from the unbreakable pull I just experienced. The thing's face peels off mine with an adhesion stronger than a tearing Band-aid. The hairs rip from my chin, cheeks, and eyebrows freely. Some even tear out of my nostrils. Tears pour out of my eyes, and I bellow, flailing my arms uselessly.

When my feet touch the ground, I fall forward against the counter, bracing myself on its edge. My whole body shakes.

"What?" I gasp. "What the hell was—"

I break off and focus on the clerk-thing. Its face is no longer mannequin-smooth. Rather, it's a cast indented with my features. The thing leans forward and crushes onto the book's blank page. Its face pours out onto the paper in delicate lines, forming the same dense script I saw on the others. I can't read a single word of it—it's in an alphabet I've never seen—but it recorded something essential about me, and I don't need to know more than that. When the ink-thing raises its head, it's only partially there, like a worn-down eraser.

It rolls its shoulders and steps over to the barrel. Gripping the cask's rim, it dips forward. The container is full of the same kind of ink its head was made of. The same kind it just filled that page with. It sticks its head to the neck in the liquid, and when it raises itself, everything has been restored to the original featureless mannequin. I'm glad I didn't drink a bunch today because I'm pretty sure I would have pissed myself more than once since I arrived here.

The clerk-thing steps into its exact original position, and its attention latches onto me. In that same almost mechanical voice, it says, "Business in The Shadowlands?"

"Oh no," I say. "I ain't going through that again."

Shadow Tommy laughs loudly and steps forward.

"Don't mind him," he says to the shadow-clerk. "It's...Doom Boy's...first time in The Shadowlands. We're here for barter."

The clerk-thing nods.

"Length?"

"Until we're done or until he's dead," Shadow Tommy says with a chuckle.

I don't think he's joking. However, the answer seems enough for the clerk. It runs its hand over the page, its fingers dripping words straight to the paper, and then it closes the book. A ripple runs across its liquid features, leaving them looking more like a resting pond than a face.

With a grunt, Shadow Tommy takes me by the elbow and walks me to the door opposite from where we entered. He gestures through, and we step out into a ramshackle town.

"Welcome to Synoro," Shadow Tommy says.

The town is built among and inside the basalt pillars. The whole place is lit by dim lanterns flickering with a pallid orange glow. Some are on posts, some are mounted to the pillars, and some glow through windows in both buildings and columns. The sky above has darkened, so their light is the only illumination.

How long were we with the clerk thing? It only felt like a few minutes.

"It's night already?" I ask.

We start toward the nearest pass between the pillars. I can't tell how big the town is because the line of sight is obstructed quickly in every direction. A few voices call here, and what I can only assume to be the shadows of a trio of small dogs run past after a rat. Whether the rat is real or the shadow of a one, I can't say.

"Time works a bit different in The Shadowlands," Shadow Tommy says. "Especially here at the edge of the civilized realm."

I nod, though he might as well have told me the sun is controlled by magical fairies. And I am pretty sure I don't have time to understand the physics of this place. There are a lot of punches I am going to have to roll with.

We pass between two especially large basalt towers and step into what looks like a small market. The space can't be more than twenty yards across, but about a dozen tables and stalls line the edges. The ground is paved with something like cobblestone. The stalls themselves are all shuttered, except for one, and empty chairs sit across covered tables. Struck by curiosity, I take one of the coverings—canvas, it feels like—and peek under the corner.

Umbrellas. A table full of umbrellas. I smirk.

"Shadows feel strongest when they're in shadow," Shadow Tommy says. "Come on. We've got places to be."

He takes my arm, but before I can move, a husky woman's voice interrupts.

"I'll bet you do."

Shadow Tommy and I both turn when she steps around from behind one of the stalls. The word "Lenses" is scrawled across its highest slat. She's not a shadow, but rather a pale-skinned woman with black eyes and hair either sandy brown or red in the dim light. The woman looks pretty young, maybe even about my age, and she's dressed in a patched-up gray coat over a tight-fit black shirt and jeans. A silver zipper runs up the center of her shirt.

"Ah, Miela." Shadow Tommy's demeanor changes in an instant. His shoulders seem to tighten, and his back stiffens.

She would have struck me as ordinary enough if I saw her back home, but she's the first person I've seen who isn't a shadow. Is that a good sign? Is she here for a reason like I am?

"We were just looking for you."

"I'll bet you were," she says. "No way you were going to head straight on through."

"Yeah, exactly. That'd be crazy," Shadow Tommy says.

Miela hasn't even looked at me. Instead, she reaches one foot forward and steps with a slightly exaggerated gate, her hands behind her back, right up beside Shadow Tommy. My companion's spine tenses even more, like he sat on a cactus.

"Definitely not something The Shadower would approve of." She raises one hand and rests it on Shadow Tommy's shoulder.

I take a step backward, trying not to jostle the umbrella table, not sure I like where this is going.

"No, definitely not," Shadow Tommy says.

"It's all about accountability, about accounting for where you are, where you've been, where you're going." Miela's grip on Shadow Tommy's shoulder tightens.

His features press together. It hurts him.

"It's about making sure he knows *how* you will pay your debts."

Miela brings her other hand from behind her back and opens it, revealing a shining, white ring. It's quite beautiful—iridescent, almost bluish purple in shimmers. Its size seems to fluctuate in her palm, and something about the way it lusters implies movement, like it's not an inanimate ring, but rather a coiled thing ready to strike.

Shadow Tommy takes a step back and waves his hands. "That's not necessary. I'm going to get—I'm going to—I'm going!"

Then, he is off running. In a blink, he's on the other side of the little market, disappearing between two basalt pillars to the right of the path we seemed to be travelling.

Miela groans and rolls her eyes before turning to face me.

*****

If Shadow Tommy runs, I run. This woman isn't good news.
Turn to page 55.

If she's from the World of Light like me, I can hurt her.
Turn to page 64.

It's a strange thing. I look at this "clerk" and something inside me wants to wither. My mouth dries out. My heartbeat reverberates, not just in my chest, but throbbing in my neck and arms. Pulses of pressure ache through my femurs.

I lick my lips, but my tongue is so dry, it's like rubber against the same. My voice cracks, and I rasp, "Danny. Danny Bradshaw."

Behind me, Shadow Tommy sucks in a sharp breath. "Oh," he says.

A ripple runs across the face of the clerk-thing. It rises.

"Danny Bradshaw," it says. "You are a person of interest in a shadow crime."

"What?" I take a step back, my shoulder jostling Shadow Tommy.

"I told you," Shadow Tommy says.

The clerk-thing dissipates like a cloud, swarms over the counter, and reforms on my side of the barrier, inches away. My heart lurches in my chest so hard, it's going to crack my ribs. Pressure swells in my head. The thing in front of me reaches with one hand through the counter, like it's not even there, and pulls an ethereal-looking book back out. It swings the binding open. While the pages flip past rapidly, I glimpse row after row of script until the movement stops.

An empty page stands open.

The clerk-thing slaps its palm to my chest. Despite my shirt, my skin grows cold and clammy. The urgency pulsing through me pulls toward its touch, and something slides from myself into its hand. Weakness surges through my limbs, and all my joints go loose. I collapse to the ground.

The clerk-thing kneels beside me and holds the book open in one hand for me to see. It slaps its other palm—the same one which touched me—to the open page. What looks like ink pours from the thing's hand onto the paper, forming words up and down the page with my name, Danny Bradshaw, in large script at the top.

My body falls into convulsions. I want to look away from the book, to gaze at Shadow Tommy or the thing that attacked me, but all I can focus on is that script on the page. It's full of symbols I can't read, other than my name. No doubt it's some sort of record of whatever crime I supposedly committed.

It doesn't really matter, I suppose. My body is getting colder, and the clerk-thing talks heatedly with Shadow Tommy in some other language.

My failure has probably caused him problems as well, but I don't know if I should feel bad since he brought me here. To be fair, I'm not sure I feel anything at all. My eyes fight to roll back.

I catch one last glimpse of the shadow-clerk standing over me, shaking its head.

"A few months in detention should soften you up for The Judge," the shadow says.

***

You chose wrong. The correct answer was I'm just going to trust Shadow Tommy's advice. Turn to page 47.

Yeah, I know a sinking ship when I see one. I can't say I trust the quality of Shadow Tommy's character, and this woman doesn't have ink for a face, but who knows what she's hiding. Shadow Tommy understands way more about this place than I do, and already, he's well out of sight.

I turn and run in the opposite direction, ducking into a narrow passage between basalt columns. It's not nearly as tight as the passages among the urchins in the Boiled Sea, so I launch right into a full sprint.

Only to skid to a stop when I curve between the next pair of columns.

There in front of me stands a towering obelisk, like the Washington Monument, except it's all carved in runes, like you'd see outside a tomb in Ancient Egypt. The structure must be twelve feet across at the base and at least a hundred feet high, probably a lot more. At each corner, a large flame dances in a wrought iron cage atop a torch, casting shadows from the carved symbols. The shadows themselves don't lie against the stonework like they should. They waft outward like cloth rustling in the wind.

A faint whispering reaches my ears. I don't know if it's just unintelligible or in a different language, but I do catch a repeated cadence reminding me almost of a poem in iambic pentameter or maybe some old church recitation. The sound is both soothing and chilling, and for half a second, I am fully entranced.

"And where do you plan to run?" Miela's voice comes from behind me. "You want to go back home and live a pointless life, apathetic, in the light of a sun that would blind you to look at it?"

I turn and take several steps backward until my heels press against the base of the monument. The stone structure isn't quite rectangular. It's shaped with a gentle concave, which leaves the torches blocking my flight to the right and left. The chant has grown louder, and I wonder vaguely if it's coming from inside the monument.

I feel compelled to turn, to reach out and press my palm to the stone. Somehow, I believe I will understand the message in the chant if I do so, but it would be insanely stupid to turn my focus away from the woman.

"Stay back." Though I'm not quite sure what I could do if she doesn't. Throw myself at her? Punch her in the face? I can't do that, right? I can't just attack someone. And if Shadow Tommy ran away, there must be more to her than meets the eye.

The voices rise in my ear sharply and fade. One of them literally passes laterally through my head, creating the Doppler effect. I twist my neck like I'm tracking a ghost speeding away. The shadows of the obelisk ruins catch my eye instead, having grown longer and larger, almost like reaching hands. Dark souls grasping from the stone.

"You're better off taking a chance with me than the stone," the woman says.

I shake my head, not wanting either, but stone and shadow can't hurt me in the way a human can, and I know it. The base of the monument has a series of lips about every two feet, so I climb up—one foot on the bottom lip, the other on the next one up. When I look down at the woman, she closes her eyes and droops her head.

Something moves in my peripheral vision.

Something dark. On both sides.

Sharp shapes like claws reach out. Curve across my field of vision. Close together like enormous hands interlocking their fingers. I can't turn my head. My body is rigid with fear. Another set of those massive talons has crossed across my torso.

A cold invasion slithers into my chest. A pain like ice erupts around my heart when the hands close in on me. My heartbeat speeds up until it's a vibration in my chest, and the pressure on it grows. I recede in my body, like I'm being pulled out of it into some place dark.

Some place enormous, some place full of an icy wind unlike any winter blast I've ever felt.

***

Wrong choice. You should have chosen If she's from the World of Light like me, I can hurt her. Turn to page 64.

I nod my head like I'm agreeing, but I'm really letting my gaze run among the basalt columns. Shadows have emerged all around us, watching with crossed arms and wary eyes. It's quite clear: If I run, they won't let me go. No doubt, they'll feed me to the void inside the pillar or some other horrible death. I suspect practically everything here can kill me in a way opposite of passing quietly in one's sleep.

"Okay, let's just get this shit show on the road," I say.

Miela smiles slightly.

On the far end of the monument clearing, the shadows part, and a hunched figure hauling some sort of two-wheeled cart by two long poles shuffles forward into the gap. Though he wears a hooded cloak, the cover has fallen from his salt and pepper hair. He is from the World of Light, like Miela and I. How many of us are here?

Unlike Miela, however, he does not have a bizarre zipper. Instead, massive bags hang underneath his eyes, dark with exhaustion. Heavy lines crow his orbital sockets and lips, and pinkish blotches mar his pale and unshaven cheeks.

When he comes to a stop, he looks up, holding his chin in defiance. Given the cloak, I almost expect him to be wearing a medieval tunic. Instead, he has on a gray and white tattered soccer jersey for a team called the Quick Hawks.

Miela steps toward him, and the bit of strength he seemed to project withers in an instant. He lowers his head like a beaten dog, hefts the poles, and trudges the cart so it faces back out the way he came.

"Who is he?" I ask.

"No one of consequence," Miela says. "Not anymore."

A little shudder rolls through the man while he waits for Miela and I to climb onboard the cart. A soft groan escapes him before he starts us in motion, when we've both been seated.

We pass among pillars of basalt. The town thins and ends, and the cart shakes and creaks over an obsidian-paved road. The columns themselves begin to diminish in height until we emerge into an open plain. A strange shimmer hangs on the land toward the horizon. The road seems to cut straight through it.

I take a deep breath.

"What is this all about? Why do I need to be a part of this?"

"It's quite simple, really," Miela says with a shrug. "No doubt, you know that in the World of Light, a great many people die in a great deal of debt. A great many debt collectors seek to pin that debt to the families of the dead. Sometimes, those families don't know better, and they agree. It's not different here. Your shadow friend convinced you to take his debt."

"No," I say. "Shadow—"

I pause. Miela has not called Shadow Tommy by his name, nor me or my brother. In fact, Miela must be her nickname, just like I am Doom Boy. Why didn't I think of something that sounded like a name, like Miela instead of Doom Boy?

I shake the thought from my head. "My brother's shadow said something like my brother had made a deal? That his shadow was part of that deal, and that if I didn't complete the deal, his shadow would pay the price."

Miela laughs. It is sharp and condescending.

"Yeah, your brother's shadow lied to you." She looks to the floor of the cart, seemingly uncomfortable. "He sold your brother's life so that he could be free of the World of Light and serve The Shadower. He'd hoped to get in my good graces and, through me, The Shadower, but I did not approve of the price he was willing to pay."

"So why are you doing this? You're not a shadow."

Miela looks ahead for a moment. I follow her gaze to the shimmer on the horizon.

Water, I realize. Flat water. The road cuts straight over it. The sun is nearly set, dim as it is, and a whole field of stars is beginning to emerge. Those same stars reflect on the water below.

"When I was a very little girl," Miela says, "my parents...died. We lived deep out in the woods, and I was left alone with their bodies. I didn't know how to get...well, anywhere, and the road intersected with a road that looked the same both ways."

"That's awful," I say.

Miela shrugs.

"It was what was in front of me. The only thing. My parents had tons of cans and boxes of food, so I just stayed there and ate while the smell came and went. I lived there for months and months, as insects and rot consumed them. I talked to them every day, even when they were nothing but bones."

I want to say something like "holy shit" or "oh my god," but nothing can capture how awful that sounds. Not even compared to losing my brother.

"You don't get into The Shadowlands without having faced something terrible," Miela says. "When I talked to the bodies of my parents, I started to hear whispers from the dark corners of my home. I thought I was going crazy, but since it was just me and the dead, I was kind of okay with that. So, I stopped talking to Mom and Dad and started talking to the voices. And the voices started telling me stories—stories about ancient kingdoms, about cataclysms, and monsters and magic.

"I was running out of food and didn't know where to go for help, and they told me they had ways to help me. That they could send me food, that they could bring me new clothes, that they could make me a doorway that would allow me to cross over to a world unlike anything I'd ever seen."

Miela looks down and seems to stare at my feet.

"I'd have died if it weren't for the messengers of The Shadower, and they showed me that I could earn my way in this world when my own world was content to let me just die. Where I could vanish in the woods unknown. That's a world where they drive away the lonely. This is a world that's drawn *to* the lonely. The Shadower was drawn to me like I was a beacon, and I will be forever grateful that he answered that call."

We ride in silence for several moments. The cart is now at the point in the road where it passes the water. The water itself is placid but totally devoid of any kind of plant life at the edges. A shoreline made only of dirt and rock.

A dull rumble rises and falls. At first, I'm not sure from where it comes, but then there's a ripple in the water around us. The surface sends concentric waves all over, densest at the shoreline. A vibration rattles through the wood of the cart beneath us. Is it a tremor? A T-rex? I wouldn't rule anything out here.

"A storm is coming," Miela says. "You're going to love this."

The horizon hides the sun completely now, and the stars gleam from a cloudless sky. It is, in fact, clearer than anything I've ever seen.

There are never this many stars at home. The purple glow of the city just buries them. Here, the stars seem brighter than The Shadowlands' sun did. They are clumped in cloudy swathes, like those pictures of the Milky Way over the desert, except instead of a single band, there are three.

The rumble comes again, louder and stronger. My teeth vibrate, and while the surface of the water ripples and splashes, a thick mist wells up. I think *steam*, but it's far too thick, denser than fog, and it hangs over the lake like an ethereal embankment not even ten feet high. It leaves only the road itself clear, other than a thin haze. The reverberations intensify. It comes from not just the ground, but the fog too.

Not fog. If a storm is coming, those are clouds.

A brilliant flash of purple lightning blasts straight up from the cloud bank, branching into the sky like a naked redwood. Farther out in the water, a second bolt launches. The thunder following the light shakes me to the bones, and I'm not even done rattling before three more bolts streak up around me.

I scream.

Miela's laughter pierces through the furor. Her head is tossed back, her grin wrought by pure glee.

"Amazing, isn't it?" she shouts. "It gets better."

The cart plods on while the lightning and thunder flash and roar around us, but never close to the road. The man pulling the vehicle wears his hood up, and his shoulders shake like he's laughing. The energy in the air stands all my hair on end and sends a metallic taste from my fillings, but it always seems far enough off, I'm not thinking I'm about to die.

A cold wind sweeps through, stirring the clouds, like fingers dragging through cotton batting.

The rain falling upward into the sky does so sparsely at first, then as heavy as a downpour. An up-pour? It flows so high I can't see the drops. Is it just launching into space? Is it going to fall back down? The lightning blossoms doubly, and now the branching grows so dense, it's like we're rolling through a forest made of light. My heart is absolutely filled with the wonder of it. I don't know how long I watch. My eyes remain wide, even as the brilliance stings them.

Muted laughter fills my ears, and it takes me a few seconds to realize it is my own. My cheeks hurt from the width of my smile.

"You act like you've never seen upward rain before," Miela shouts.

It really is amazing, the most awesome thing I've ever seen, and it's the only time since Shadow Tommy brought me here I've not felt like I was about to be killed.

It only lasts a few minutes. The storm dies almost as fast as it began, and then the air above the water is empty and still. My heart calms with it. The only thing that lasts is the icy wind. I shiver fiercely, rubbing my arms to try to keep warm. My skin is a little numb by the time the water around us ends and the moon begins to rise—a radiant pearl bigger than any night moon I've ever seen.

We ease to a stop. The man pulling us sets down his poles, and the cart rocks forward. He draws his hands to his lips and breathes into them. His knees creak up and down slowly. They're excessively stiff, and he groans softly while he does so.

I feel so selfish to have ridden in the cart all this time, with him doing such hard work. And I didn't even think about who he is. Damn. Why didn't I get out and walk?

The man cries out and jerks his foot in a wild, sideways arc. He wobbles precariously and grunts hard twice.

The man bellows with pain and drops to one knee, grabbing at his ankle. Miela stares at him, her jaw set, and then begins to scan the area around him.

"What is it?" I rise from the cart's bench.

"Help me!" he howls.

The man swats at something on the ground. His hand jerks up, and he shrieks anew, gripping his wrist and arching his back. He slumps against the cart, and the whole thing lurches up for a moment. The axle creaks at the torque.

I look to Miela, but she's staring at the man, her face locked in steely resolve. She isn't going to help him, but I don't know why. The man thrashes his arms and heaves his torso. Desperation chisels his every feature.

Was this what Tommy looked like when he drowned in the pool?

There isn't any question: I have to help him.

*****

Grab the man's arms and pull him onto the cart by heaving backward. Turn to page 72.

Climb off the cart and shove him in. Turn to page 74.

Without hesitation, I lunge forward, trying to envision myself grabbing the girl by the wrist, twisting it behind her back, and driving her downward with my weight while I hook my foot in front of her ankle. I have absolutely no training in any kind of fighting whatsoever, but the sequence of movements is so perfectly clear in my mind, my body can match it.

My hand closes on her arm.

Kind of.

My thumb doesn't quite manage to make it, landing sideways on her skin. My fingers find a moment of purchase, but when I attempt to twist her arm around her body, the grip fails, and she spins away. Her other arm swings into a tight fist, which hammers me right in the temple. Spots flash in my vision, and I stagger sideways, crashing into the stall beside her. I bang my hip on the wooden edge and yelp.

My side aches and my temple throbs, but it's the derisive laugh she gives that really hurts.

I teeter but don't fall, and while I orient toward her, she reaches up to the zipper of her shirt. My hands get clammy. Even kind of delirious—maybe *because* I'm kind of delirious—I wonder if she's about to take her top off. I have not even had a girlfriend, so I'm not exactly used to people opening their clothes in front of me.

However, when she pulls the zipper down, she doesn't just remove her shirt. She pulls away the whole front of her body, exposing a gaping cavity. In the darkness, a pocket too large to be the inside of a human, rests a small platform holding an old-fashioned scale. On one side rests a small stack of golden weights, and on the other, a shadow in the shape of a beating heart.

What in the hell am I looking at?

Miela reaches inside herself and plucks what almost looks like a string from the beating shadow heart. Then, quickly and confidently, she steps toward me and presses the shadow string to my chest, like she's forcing a dowel rod onto me which suddenly comes to life like a writhing snake.

I look down in horror when it pierces my shirt and burrows straight through my skin between my ribs. A sucking sensation spreads around it as if my body is pulling it in. My breathing accelerates. I jerk the neck of my shirt down to expose my breast, throw my hand against my skin, and try to grab it, but it's like my fingers close on nothing, even while it drives into me.

"Just stay calm." Miela zips herself back up.

"Screw that," I shriek.

Miela just pulled her skin back on. She's like a living pair of goddamn jeans.

"It won't hurt you."

"Fuck you!" I drag my fingernails across my chest and over my heart. The hole it tunneled into closes behind it. "Fuck this."

"So imaginative." Miela reaches out and flicks her index finger down my cheek, almost like she's trying to light a match.

My patchy stubble stings in the wake of her touch.

"What the hell is it?" I ask. When I look down, my skin is completely healed. A strange chill sits against my heart, but otherwise, it would be easier to believe I hallucinated the whole ordeal.

Maybe I *did*. Hell, perhaps I am crouched in some corner at the funeral home, suffering a psychotic break. Mom and Dad are probably shaking me and yelling in my ears to snap out of it.

Mom and Dad.

I stiffen, eyes wide.

Since I came here, I've hardly thought of them. The guilt of Tommy's death resurges: my embarrassment about how I broke their trust, the terror of walking back through the door of their house, having to live as their child every day.

"How much do you know about why you're here?"

I shake my head.

"Figures. That little chickenshit couldn't be straightforward if he waited atop the Gissu gallows for his body to drop into the noose." She stares at the ground by my feet for a moment. Her mouth and head move, as if she's silently talking something over with herself. Miela looks up. "But I'm not like him, you see. I'm not trying to save my own neck. I have a job, and my job is simply to help you do your Shadow Friend's job. Come with me."

She sweeps her hand upward, palm to the sky, toward a gap between the basalt columns opposite the direction in which Shadow Tommy fled. The flickering light is a bit brighter through that passage, and she starts off without further comment.

With no way to find Shadow Tommy, I might as well follow her. It bothers me to think that, but I can't seem to override the thought. Just trying to brush it aside sends a chill through my heart.

On the other side of the passage, we stop before what I can only describe as an obelisk—a lot like the Washington Monument, except carved all over with symbols which remind me of hieroglyphics. Torches at each corner of the monument toss dancing shadows off the symbols, but these shadows have body, like Shadow Tommy. The symbols are alive and immediately whisper to me. Straight into my heart. I want to reach out and press my palm to the stone, but when I take a step forward, Miela places a hand to my chest. Her touch is strangely warm and instantly comforting.

"Do not approach," she says.

Miela nudges me backward. I resist for a moment but then relent. The relief of obedience is palpable.

The strange thread of shadow...The way it burrowed into my heart...I forgot it just happened.

"What did you do to me?"

Miela hesitates and runs her eyes up the obelisk.

"Before I say any more, I must know, do you serve The Unlucky Number or The One Who Trusts the Dark?"

I look at her. The oil on her skin lusters in the shifting light, and a breeze rustles her hair. The question is obviously some kind of test, but I'm really not even sure to whom she is referring.

Shadow Tommy mentioned them briefly, but I know next to nothing other than that he seemed kind of hostile toward them. I also don't know that I should be on Shadow Tommy's side. Despite the fact his warnings kept me alive, he ditched me pretty quick.

"I don't know," I say. "Neither."

Miela nods.

"I can work with that." She points at the monolith. "This is the marker of Aurelio the Defiant, the last great king who passed into the endless shadow, hoping to undo the banishment of The One Who Trusts the Dark."

It occurs to me she hasn't answered my original question, but the thought is hard to hold onto, like something inside doesn't want me to think too hard on it. Like the thing she put there wants me to focus on something else. On the other hand, I realize The One Who Trusts the Dark must be the same as The Eater of the Light.

"What happened to him?"

Miela shrugs.

"He couldn't overcome the will of The Thirteen. But his attempt left a rent in the fabric of The Shadowlands. Any shadow who gets too close is pulled into the embrace of the beyond nothing. It would rip your shadow right out of you."

"Shouldn't they put up a guardrail or something?'

"The monument *is* the guardrail. They built the monument around the rent to prevent shadows from approaching, but its influence has grown over the centuries. Now your shadow will feel its pull from even a couple steps closer than we are."

"I mean, a little caution tape—"

She brushes my words away, and the wave of her hand shuts my mouth like I'm a ventriloquist dummy. On the other side of the obelisk, a couple of shadows stand at the far end of the clearing, watching us with curiosity.

"I plan to bring you to a young shadow man named Little Bit. He is not far from here. I need you to convince him to come with you."

I want to chuckle at the name, but I gave mine as "Doom Boy."

It doesn't look so funny anymore.

"So that he can be sucked into the hole in the universe?" I ask. "I'm not sure I'm okay with that."

"So that he can stand before The Judge. He is a criminal that has committed many crimes against Shadow Law. If he is found guilty, then, and only then, will he be committed to the rent."

"Don't you have jails or something?"

Miela locks me with a hard look. There are a great many more shadows watching now from all the channels between the basalt pillars.

"You are in the World of Shadows," Miela says. "And I have no doubt your Shadow Friend got you to make a deal. Like it or not, you are bound to see that deal through. This is my only offer to help. Say no, and you will stand in violation of your deal."

I don't want to break my deal, and I have no idea who I'm actually looking for, other than their name being "Little Bit," which I suspect won't do me a whole lot of good if no one uses their real names. However, whatever this woman did to me seems to give her some ability to influence how I react.

If I don't get away now, I don't know I'll ever be able to try again.

*****

"Okay. Let's just get this shit show on the road." Turn to page 58.

Yeah, I'll just make my own way thank you very much. Turn to page 69.

I take a step to the side, putting a little bit of a gap between myself and her. Though it seems like she might have some sort of influence on me through whatever that shadow thing is, I don't know if she can directly stop me. But I'm sure as hell not going to obey someone who stuffed their chest with a pair of scales floating in an abyss. I shouldn't have trusted Shadow Tommy as far as I did either. Maybe I should have just stayed in my coffin and let myself die. At least I could have demanded to be sent back. I didn't attempt to take control of my situation. All I've done since I came here is try not to die.

"Yeah, the thing is," I say, "I'm not saying no. I'm saying I'm not doing this with *you*. I don't trust you. I don't trust anyone here."

Miela presses her lips together, and her cheeks flush. Her eyes narrow.

"You've seen some dangerous stuff since you've been here, yeah?" she asks, venom in her voice.

An aura of hostility radiates from her, like she's a balloon inflated until you see through the skin. I take another sideways step, but in my peripheral vision, multiple shadows stand in each path among the basalt columns. A crowd has formed, and by the way they glance from Miela to me, I gather they're here to help her. I'm trapped in the monument clearing.

"Yeah," I answer hesitantly. "A flying beast, massive urchins, hypnotic water, that thing in the border checkpoint...I don't like this place. I don't want anything to do with this place."

Miela spits at my feet.

"You think we want anything to do with the likes of you? The way you just throw your shadow to the ground as if it's only fit to step on? You didn't care if you had a shadow or not until you were brought here. Have you ever even wondered who your shadow is?"

"I-I-I—" I stammer, but the question has thrown me off.

The likes of me? She looks like she's from my world.

Of course, I've never wondered who my shadow is. It's me. But Shadow Tommy's shadow isn't him, is it? It sure hasn't seemed a whole lot like Tommy ever was. If Tommy sold out his shadow, though, did I even really know him?

"That's the thing about you casters," Miela says. "You don't try to see through *anyone* else's eyes. It's all just *me, me, me, I, I, I.*"

"I'm sorry? I—"

"See, the thing is..." Miela stomps toward me. "The thing is, I can't just force you to comply. This had to be a willing choice. *Had* to be."

Something catches in her voice. Sadness. Regret. She looks down and to the left, then nods slightly to herself. When she raises her chin and faces me, her mouth is a slit, and her eyes are dead as onyx.

Oh, boy. I think I fucked up.

"I can only hide the hole in your heart so much," Miela says. "It's just easier to pull my finger from the dam and find someone else."

Miela's hand snaps to my throat. Her grip is brutal, like there are barbs in her fingers and palm which hook into my skin. Hot blood bursts all up and down my neck where she squeezes. With her other hand, she reaches to her own throat and unzips herself for a second time. I try to fight, but every move tears my skin further, and the agony of it leaves my head spinning.

With a steady, robotic motion, Miela pulls my head toward the gaping hole she opened in her chest. The darkness is inside, and so are the scales, but now they're swarming with black insects. The shadows of roaches, wasps, spiders, centipedes. The scales swing up and down when their mass shifts from one platform to the next. The largest centipedes in the batch rise to meet my entering face.

Their prickly feet jab into my cheeks and pull away, stab and jerk back.

The zipper slides up on its track, closing against my neck.

My body thrashes outside hers, but the walls of her insides press against my head, immobilizing it, like it's caught in the gears of some unbreakable machine. Darkness engulfs me, but I still hear the squelches of the bugs crawling over each other and the clicking of their mandibles until the moment my ears are blocked by the pressure of the closing space.

White lighting of agony explodes all through my cranium. Bone fractures and crashes, and the last thought I have is that what's inside my skull is about to burst out of my face, to land in front of the scales for the bugs to feast upon.

***

You chose wrong. The correct choice was "Okay. Let's just get this shit show on the road." Turn to page 58.

He has to get off the ground fast because whatever hurt him is still down there. I lunge forward and close both my hands around the man's wrist. His feet kick hard against the dirt, and his weight rises like he's about to throw himself into the cart, aided by my pull.

"I got you," I shout, even while the cart's weight shifts and my knees wobble.

The man's legs give out entirely, like a marionette whose strings were cut. His mass crashes down, his ribs deflect off the lip of the cart, and his hip bangs into one of the poles. The only reason he doesn't fall prone is because I manage to keep my grip. I heave, and the effort sends the air rushing from my lungs.

"Help me," I croak, throwing a glance to Miela, but she's slumped back in her seat, her face red.

She's looking off to the side and biting her lower lip. The injured man shrieks, and his whole body goes into devastating convulsions, bucking like a mechanical bull. Something pops in his arm, and his shoulder goes all right angled in absolutely the wrong way.

"Oh god," I shout, but I don't let go. This is the closest I'll ever come to having another chance to save Tommy. I can barely hold on, for as hard as he flings his weight about, but I clench like he's the one keeping *me* from falling to my own death.

Something beneath me cracks with a sharp report. My feet drop through the cart bottom when the board under me breaks, and my body plummets. The board buckles upward as I fall, and the jagged splinter drives straight up into me, where my thigh meets my hip. The fracture of my pelvis sounds when the wedge drives deeper inside me, and then the whole world goes white with a depth of pain I never imagined possible. A churning, roiling ring fills my ears, and something in my brain locks up.

I process nothing, and then I am nothing.

***

Wrong choice. The correct answer was Climb off the cart and shove him in. Turn to page 74.

The man reaches his hand towards me, but I hesitate, thinking again of Tommy. Of sinking. Don't let drowning people just grab you. Put your arm around them, or they pull you under. I wouldn't call myself weak, but I'm not especially strong. So, I am not sure I'll be able to hoist him up, not safely on a wobbly cart anyway. Even now, the wheels creak on their axle when our weight shifts. I need my feet on the ground to be able to use my weight the way I need to.

Without letting myself think any further, I leap off the cart. The ground beneath me crunches. Does obsidian make that sound? My shoes are sticky while I lurch over to the man. It's like I've stepped into superviscous mud or taffy...or something. The ground is not writhing, I tell myself. It is *not* writhing.

I stomp as I walk. The squelching crunch grows thicker, stickier, and moister with each step. When I'm right beside the man, I don't hesitate to clasp both of my hands as hard into his cloak as I can. The shirt under it bunches up in my grip too, and I hope that'll be enough. I hurl up and forward with every bit of strength I have.

The man's weight lurches, and his chest lands half on the cart. His arms crack against the wood. I brace myself to catch his falling weight, but his arms jerk outward and grab a hold of the cart's lip. His muscles bulge, and his tendons stand out.

I stomp my feet again. Fresh crunches like some beast gnashing on splintering bones...

The ground *isn't* swimming with shadow scorpions. Nope. I'm just stepping on someone's spilled candy. Yep, that's it. The ones I've crushed *aren't* still writhing against my shoes. Nope. The ones whose bodies are crushed but stingers are intact aren't still trying to sting the sides of my shoes. Nope...

I heave the man's weight again. His arms desperately claw forward until he pulls himself entirely into the cart. I leap up beside him onto Miela's side, my face right up in hers while I brace myself. The whole cart teeters precariously under our combined weight. Miela cries out and flings herself toward the other side. The shift in weight lets the lifted wheel crash back down with a jolt.

The man grunts in his throat, a fat, syrupy sound. His face is all blotchy red and webbed with purple veins. Is he dying? The tendons in his neck are taut, and his cheeks and lips are pulled down in a hideous grimace. Blood smears his teeth and gums.

Out of breath, I rasp, "Is he going to be okay?"

Miela shrugs.

"If he makes it through the next few minutes, he should be fine. The venom is short-lasting."

I brace my feet so they're steady and straighten my shoulders.

"You were going to let him die."

"I'm not allowed to intervene," Miela says. "Even if it means he dies and we walk."

"Who the hell is going to see? We're in the middle of..." I pause and look around. "Whatever freakshow of a wasteland this is."

Miela grits her teeth.

"Not all prisons have walls," she growls. "And not everything that watches has eyes."

That last part sends a chill down my body. It reminds me of the saying "God is always watching," but it feels more imminently real. This is the land of upward rain and floating, sideways lakes. Who knows what's possible here. My shoulders slump.

"What did he do?"

"He broke a deal to The Shadower," Miela says. "He betrayed a courier and damaged The Shadower's trade."

With a sigh, I pull the man's legs fully into the cart and do my best to arrange him more comfortably. His breathing is jagged, and he whimpers, but he's not conscious.

"And this is the punishment?"

"Deals are sacred here. Trust is precious; therefore, it's the most valuable currency."

"What the hell kind of place is this?"

"What kind of place is the World of Light?" Miela asks. "I'm one of a few people born in that world who has lived nearly their whole life in The Shadowlands, but I can tell you that judging it based on what you've seen is like judging your world by a walk across a few miles of Antarctica."

I sit quietly and think about that. Shadow Tommy said he brought me in off the beaten path. Does The Shadowlands have their version of a big border crossing like in Texas or an international airport like DFW? If The Shadowlands is separate from my world but somehow adjacent, are there other worlds which cross with it? How far am I really from home?

I wrap my arms around my knees and wonder what my parents are doing. Did they tear the funeral home apart looking for me, or did they just mutter some swears and call the police, to have them do the searching? Was Mom upset I was gone? Was Dad? Are they planning to put my picture on telephone poles, or have they just written me off too? Glad to be done with the kid who let their real child drown? They never thought I would pull myself together and become anything. Who knows. Maybe they are right.

If I come back, will they ever trust me again? How can they? Can I offer them a deal that will let me act like their son again? I've hardly thought about them since I got here. How can their son go so long without thinking about how he destroyed the family, even in the midst of danger? The guilt sloshes about inside me and seeps over in tears, like I'm a glass a little too full.

"Guilt is a liability here," Miela says. "It's a parasite. It'll suck you dry, and scavengers will pick apart your bones."

"So The Shadowlands *do* have something in common with the World of Light," I say with a smirk.

"At least you're alive now," Miela says softly. "Alive and shadowed."

"Right."

We sit quietly for a couple of moments. The darkness weighs on me. There are no insects calling, just the low moan of the wind.

"We need to sleep," Miela says. "We'll move on in the morning."

My stomach rumbles. It strikes me just how parched my throat is.

"I'm hungry and thirsty," I say.

Miela grunts and reaches beneath the cart's bench, opening a small compartment. She pulls out a canteen and hands it over. I take it and raise it to my lips. When I take the liquid into my mouth, I catch a whiff of the pungent, fishy contents.

I spit out what hits my tongue before I even register how brackish it tastes. The aftertaste swarms my mouth, and I sputter and gag. It's like I sucked on a rotting anchovy.

"Like it or not, that's all you're getting until morning," Miela says.

"What the hell is it?"

"Black water. It's what shadows drink. It won't quench your thirst, but it'll make your throat feel wet."

"This place sucks."

We fall into silence, and soon, Miela snores softly. Most folks look more peaceful when they sleep, but she just appears worried. I try to make myself comfortable, but no matter how I settle down, the angles of the cart press into my muscles and joints.

During the waking stretches between fits and bursts of light sleep, I wonder again if my parents are scared that I'm not home. That is all they need, for the "other kid" to add more stress to their lives. FML. The glimpses of dreams I get thrust Tommy, Mom, and Dad front and center: images of their faces, of them at the funeral, of Tommy drowning again and again.

When the sky begins to lighten a deep red horizon, I'm ready to sit up and get the hell on with it. I focus on Miela's watchful gaze.

"You didn't sleep much," she says.

"Was thinking about my parents. That they must be going crazy."

"They've hardly thought about you." I wince, but her expression softens, and she continues, "Just like you hardly thought about them much yesterday. They don't even really know you're missing."

"I disappeared during their other child's funeral."

"Yeah, and they'll tell themselves that you slipped off to go spend some time with a friend. They'll even think they remember you telling them you planned to do just that."

"But I didn't," I protest.

"The Shadowlands...protects itself. It doesn't want to be discovered by the World of Light, not by the bulk of it anyway. When folk have reason to find it, it turns their minds away and helps them rationalize it. It's just like his family." Miela points to the driver. "They think he disappears on drinking binges and that he's checked himself into rehab alternately when he's gone for three days. Sometimes, he believes it himself."

Maybe because we are talking about him or perhaps just because we *are* talking, the man groans. His breath wheezes, something rattling thickly in his chest. He breaks into a hacking cough, which leaves a string of mucus stretching from his lip. Feebly, he wipes his mouth with the back of his hand and opens his eyes. They look cloudy and dull, and his skin is ashen around them.

"Time to get us moving," Miela says softly.

The man grunts and manages the slightest of nods.

I shake my head. Even though I haven't been in The Shadowlands long enough to know how things work here and haven't seen many people in seriously bad health, it's clear the man is way too sick.

"His damn arms are gonna fall off if he tries," I say.

Miela shrugs. "And if so, that's just part of the price he has to pay."

A massive weight drags the man's features down. The muscles around his eyes tremble, like he's holding back tears. There's a cruelty to this place I just can't handle. How can anybody? How can Miela be so calm? How is anything going to change if no one does the right thing?

*****

Miela is set on this. Let the man pull the cart. Turn to page 21.

To hell with Miela. The man must rest. Climb down and pull the cart. Turn to page 84.

I push his hand down and pull myself onto my knees in the coffin. The wind is even steadier when I am upright, and my hair ripples. Goosebumps rise underneath my jacket sleeves. The gale whistles through all the narrow paths and slots among the quartz urchins, or whatever they are. If the sun provides any warmth, it's not landing in this spot. The landscape around me is so alien, though. If I weren't so damn cold, I wouldn't even believe it was real.

"Where the hell am I?" I ask.

"We've got to get moving," Tommy's shadow insists. He looks about nervously. His gaze dances over the rock field. "It's not safe."

"Not safe *how*?" I ask. "This is bullshit. If you're really Tommy's shadow, then you've seen most of the same movies I have, and you and I both know how annoying it is to say, 'Oh, there's no time to answer simple questions.'"

Shadow Tommy presses a hand to the casket's side. He appears to be searching the ground around the display platform, though I can't actually make out his eyes moving.

"The Shadowlands doesn't work like a movie," Shadow Tommy says. "It doesn't work like your world. Tommy's world." The dark facsimile of my brother kneels and puts his hand to the platform. His cheeks drop, and a smile falls onto his lips. He shakes his head and says softly, "Too late."

I press my own hand to the casket's lid. A soft vibration tickles my palm, intensifying and buzzing into my kneecaps through the velvet padding. It's a strange thrum boring straight to the marrow of my bones. My teeth ring. An itch flares in both my ears, like there's a knot of bees inside my skull.

The whole coffin wobbles when my weight shifts. The vibration escalates to actual shaking, and an earthquake seems to be welling straight beneath me. Thunder fills the air, growing louder until the whole world roars.

Shadow Tommy falls to the ground and scrambles frantically between the quartz urchins. A huge fissure opens the earth beneath him. I reach to grab the edge of the coffin, steadying myself so I can climb down, but rock, dirt, and shards burst straight from the ground, driven by a massive black shape. All I have time to make out are enormous jaws opening wide when I'm thrown from atop the coffin.

The jaws snap shut just after my feet pass through them, and I am clear, sailing through the air. My arms pinwheel, and my legs kick as if they have minds of their own. My arc peaks, and I plunge toward the quartz urchins. Toward those sharp needles sticking out in all directions.

I throw my arms in front of my face and draw my knees to my chest before colliding with one of the outcroppings. Its needles plunge into my body—one through my left thigh, one straight through my abdomen below my belly button, and a third through my right breast. Everything becomes a white-light sea of pain.

My momentum lurches to a stop, and denser and shorter spikes pierce up and down my arms, legs, and torso. One of them punches through my teeth and into the back of my throat. Another buries itself into my cheek bone. I don't know if it went deep enough to pierce my brain, but the agony lights my whole body in a totality I never imagined.

Blackness overtakes me and silence prevails.

***

The correct answer was to take his hand. "You'd better explain soon." Turn to page 9.

I take a step towards the shadow boy and girl but hesitate. It's just too perfect a setup to be believed. There haven't been any other shadows here. We haven't seen a single one since the border town. No doubt, there are shadow folk who live here and there, but now we're on a desolate road, only stalled this long because the cart man got injured, and we just happen to cross paths with an injured child? Back in my world, folks play injured all the time to lure in kind-hearted people. Then they jack their car or stab them and steal their phones.

"Maybe you're right," I say over my shoulder.

I turn around. The cart man is lifting the poles. He's letting his hood hang down lower than ever, and I can't even see his face.

"What are you doing?" I ask.

The man just grunts and shakes his head.

"Going around." There's something final in his voice that tells me he's taking back cart duty and pivoting it. He's trying to keep his face hidden from the kids.

When the cart grumbles into the road around the far side of the rock rise, the little shadow boy stands.

"Hey!" he shouts. "Where do you think you're going?"

The prone girl raises her head. "I need help!"

My eyes widen. Even in the dim light and early long shadows, I make out something dripping rapidly from her chin to the glass pebbles below. The fluid accelerates and begins to run as a thin, unbroken stream. Is that blood? Is her face *pouring* blood? I run my foot through the glass again. She really is hurt.

"Stop," I yell to the cart man, but he shakes his head slightly, digs in his heels, and pushes harder.

In doing so, his hood falls back around his shoulders, exposing his salt and pepper hair and all those aged lines.

The little boy gasps.

"Journeyman?"

The man cringes and lowers his chin, as if he wants to pull his head back inside his upper body.

"Holy shit, it's Journeyman!" the shadow boy shouts.

The little shadow girl pushes herself up. In her hand, she clutches a long blade of jagged glass. It has to be cutting into her hand real bad, but she doesn't seem to care. She strides at the cart man, her arms swinging, her face full of angry purpose. If she wasn't a child, she would be utterly terrifying. Hell, even as a child, she's pretty damn scary.

A clatter echoes from somewhere above. Five more shadow children stand at the top of the rocks. Two of them hold what look like clubs, and a couple more clutch what seem to be blades. All the weapons are jet black, like they were pulled right from the shadows themselves.

"Gut him!" the first shadow boy calls after the shadow girl.

"Cut him to pieces!" one of the shadows on the rocks yells.

The little girl shadow is almost to Journeyman, but he is hardly even reacting. All he does is hang his head a little.

"Don't hurt him," I yell at the little girl, but she doesn't answer.

She's about to pass right by me.

*****

Grab a hold of her and pull the knife away so you can find out what's going on. Turn to page 90.

According to Miela, you can die but the cart man can't. Don't get involved. Turn to page 95.

Make note of this choice at the front of the book or on a scrap paper with your other choices.

Right there, I want to hit Miela. I won't because I suspect that, if I try, she's going to unzip herself and let a bunch of jackals or something loose from the void in her chest. The only thing I can think of is when I saw Tommy get pushed around by the bullies at the bus stop on the corner near our house.

That was a few years ago, when I had the hardest time getting myself to do anything once I was home from school, but that day, I ran out the front door so fast, I didn't even bother to put my shoes on. Those little assholes saw me tearing across the lawn in a full sprint. Maybe if they had not been caught off guard, they would have kicked the crap out of me, but they scattered in a heartbeat. It was one of the best feelings I ever had.

That's how bad things stop. And maybe it's because the man forced the image of Tommy drowning into my mind when he was being stung, but I feel the same kind of protectiveness now.

However, I don't hit Miela. What I do is hop right off that cart and step between the poles.

"Please, it's my duty," the man says.

I look back over my shoulder.

"Tell me your name," I say.

But the man shakes his head, so I shrug and raise the cart. I plant my heels hard against the obsidian road and shove myself forward. The whole cart groans, and the wheels squeak.

Something clatters below.

I look down to my feet. Chips of obsidian lift, and black scorpions crawl out from little holes beneath. With a gasp, I lurch forward harder and crush my stepping foot down on an emerging scorpion. With the next step, I smush another, then one more.

"You need to stop right now," Miela says.

"Please," the man adds. "It's the law."

I bend my head down and watch the arachnids emerging around me. Even if I wanted to stop, if I do, they'll be upon me in a moment, jabbing their venom through my skin with their stingers.

"To hell with this place," I say. "To hell with the law. It's a bullshit law."

I pump my legs as hard as I can. The cart rattles behind me like thunder and rolls easier as it accelerates. I'm so proud of myself for not just watching that man suffer. My muscles burn from the strain, but I don't care. It's the first time I've not felt guilty since Tommy died.

When finally my breath runs out, I'm positively glowing. My cheeks are hot and flushed, and I look back over my shoulder, full of smug satisfaction.

Miela and the weary man both scowl at me.

"You're going to have to answer for this when you face The Judge," she says.

"You know what my teacher told me in school? That an unjust law is not a law."

"All laws serve those who make them," Miela says. "Shadow laws especially."

The man sighs like he's carrying ten thousand pounds. He deserves a chance to rest. It's not like he killed someone. I adjust my grip on the cart poles and check the road, but it seems like I'm clear of the scorpions. Still, though I have some energy left, I take up a slower pace. I don't know how far to our destination, but I'm sure there's plenty of ground to cover.

The road veers off to the right, rising along a slight incline. The flat, almost featureless landscape takes on a rockier, more jagged feel, and soon, the road winds among crags. The slope increases a bit too, and the work becomes substantially more strenuous.

I'm too out of shape to keep it up for long. When a fork looms ahead, I'm already huffing and puffing. As I approach the divergence, I look left and right down the paths. The road seems to curve away around the same peak of stone and rejoin at the other end. On the right side, the obsidian seems a bit more broken, a bit more jagged, while to the right, a dark shape lies in the road.

No, *two* dark shapes.

Two figures, one hunched over the other. The second lies prone and motionless. I can't be certain from where I stand, but they seem to be children. I set the poles down and look back to Miela.

"I'm going to check it out," I say.

"Don't. This could be a trap. Take the broken road."

The upright kid looks back over its shoulder. It's a shadow, but I'm too far away to make out any other features.

"Hey!" the kid says, jumping up and waving their arms. "Hey! Come quick! She fell!"

Miela mouths the word *no* at me.

Are they kidding, or what?

I step away from the cart and toward them.

*****

They're kids and they need help. Turn to page 87.

You can't trust anything here. Take the broken road.
Turn to page 82.

The shadow boy looks back towards me. I think he's a boy anyway. The sun still isn't very high up, and the rocks block a lot of the early light, throwing long shadows. The ground alongside the road is made of some sort of strange gravel. I drag the toe of my shoe through it when I take my next step. The bits of gravel scatter and tumble with a clatter, reflecting the light.

Glass. Glass beads. Some intact, some pulverized into splinters and shards, some nothing but a fine powder.

I don't want to inhale that. A puff of the glass dust rises from my shoe. I stop dragging my foot and set my next step flatly, more carefully.

The child ahead is lying prone, though. They must have their face right in it. Are they sucking the glass in through their nose? Is it in their mouth? Their eyes? God, I'd hate to try to blink out the slivers and shards. It would be like having tiny needles in my eyes. It does, however, make me wonder if there is actually anything I can do to help.

I step forward cautiously. They may be kids, but little kids can be nasty too. Especially if they're acting as bait for a trap laid by bigger kids. I peer among the cracks and boulders. Nothing seems to move in the shadows, other than a few long shadowy grasses I understand to be the shadows of plants. I listen for whispering voices. For clatters of rock. For joints popping because they have been crouched in wait.

Nothing.

"Come on," the shadow boy says. "Come on and help. She's really hurt."

On the cart behind me, Miela is standing at attention on the seat. She's watching much more closely whether or not something is coming up from behind to trap us in. The way I see it, if we *are* about to be trapped, I would rather be attempting to do the right thing when it happens, not letting what looks like a little girl die. The cart man shrinks back in his seat, pulling the hood of his cloak over his head so it hangs down and covers much of his face.

I continue forward. Part of me wants to rush, to acknowledge the kid's urgency. No doubt, he's hating how slow I'm moving, and I can't help feeling a little icky inside for taking my time. But the fact is, it *has* been dangerous here. As much as I'd like to do the right thing, I have been one decision away from death every step of the way.

When I get close enough, the little shadow boy stands up and steps out of the way. He wrings his hands around a length of rope seemingly sewn into his shirt. He twists it, his otherwise young shadow face etched deep with lines. Even though the tones are practically black on black, his eyes are obviously large. They flit back and forth from me to his companion.

I drop to one knee and lay my hand on the back of her shoulder.

"Hey," I say softly, feeling stupid because, no doubt, the little boy has been trying to get her to acknowledge his voice since well before I came up. "I'm going to turn you over."

I firm my grip and pull slowly. The shoulder rises, but her other bends the wrong way, making it hard to pivot. With a tug, I get her on her side. Black fluid pours from her eye sockets and nose, a little clatter among the glass debris. A heavy grimace twists the bottom half of her face, and she spits a mouthful of blood, which probably contains more glass, in one great glut spattering across several inches.

My stomach turns at the sight. I wish I had eaten something. I'm not easily grossed out, but her blood is black, thick, and stringy.

The little boy takes a step toward the cart, his head cocked. No doubt, he is wondering why the others are not helping too. I wouldn't mind knowing the same, but I don't think empathy or sympathy have a lot of presence in The Shadowlands.

"What happened to you?" I ask softly.

She groans through a mouthful of bloody sludge.

Behind me, the shadow boy says, "Journeyman?"

The little girl's eyes pop open.

Miela says, "Oh hell."

The injured shadow girl rocks flat onto her back. I try to catch her before her head grinds into the glass, but her other arm comes swinging up, as if it's just carrying on her momentum. My head turns toward it just in time to prevent the dagger-like shard of glass she holds from jamming straight into my ear. It jams into my eye instead.

There's a crunch of bone when the shadow girl twists the shard and shoves it a bit deeper through my eye socket.

***

You chose wrong. You should have chosen You can't trust anything here. Take the broken road.

Turn to page 82.

Just when the girl passes me, I lash out and grab her by the wrist of the arm holding the jagged glass blade. She pivots to the side and hisses at me, her shadow teeth black against the cavern of her mouth. Her eyes are fierce, a dark ring set against black, with only the slightest differences in shade to make them visible. For a split second, she is frozen and quivering with anger.

The girl couldn't be more than ten. She's too small to be dangerous.

The blade falls from her hand, black blood rushing out from where it had been pressed into her flesh, only to be gripped by her waiting other hand. She clenches it hard enough, the glass grinds against bone, and she drives it upward through my arm. It pierces right between the two bones of my forearm, and my hand releases her instantly.

I scream when the point sticks out from my muscle, just as she snaps the blade to the side with force beyond what her little body should be capable of. It shatters inside my arm.

My limb becomes a living thing of roaring pain, and I flail it blindly in the air, staggering sideways. My feet catch on the uneven ground, and I trip. When my head hits the gravel, my temple strikes stone with a crunching squelch. A massive wave of nausea and dizziness overwhelms me, and the whole world spins like a carnival ride.

Somewhere in the chaos, something grips at my torso, at my shirt, tearing downward so my chest is exposed.

My heart pounds against my ribs, like a prisoner thrashing against the door of a tiny jail. It knows what is coming. Sees what I can't.

The split second of pain when something pierces my chest between my third and fourth ribs is so fast, it's like getting a flu vaccine from a fast-handed pharmacist. What happens in my heart is fireworks inside me. Burning. Searing. Explosive.

Then, silence and dark.

*****

You chose wrong. The correct answer was According to Miela, you can die but the cart man can't. Don't get involved.

Turn to page 95.

As discreetly as I can, I back up along the road to where the little boy disappeared. His companions all seem quite focused on Miela and the little girl, and they don't so much as turn their heads at me when my feet lightly scuff through the glass beads. I get closer to a hollow among the rocks leading into the throat of a narrow tunnel. Just inside, stalactites and stalagmites make the opening appear like a stone mouth. I creep at a steady pace until I'm able to entirely duck out of sight among the boulders. A cold wind blows from the opening like a breath.

I glance back. The other shadows have tightened their distance from Miela and the little girl, and their backs are all to me. I peer into the cave's darkness. The little boy can be standing right in the cave's mouth and be all but invisible. I edge forward among the teethlike stones, half expecting the cave to suddenly clamp down and devour me. At this point, I've honestly seen stranger things in this place.

I pause among the deep shadows, trying to let my eyes adjust, wondering what Tommy thought of The Shadowlands. What parts did he see? Did he witness things like the floating lake? Did he feel the siren song of the sideways waterfall in his bones, like I did? What would Mom and Dad think if I told them about this?

Based on what Miela said, they would probably brush it off as me being crazy with grief over Tommy, or maybe they would just dismiss it altogether. Say it was the meaningless daydreams of a pointless child. Sometimes, I wonder if they would rather I just cease to exist. Maybe I can go deep inside that cave and never come out.

My heart grows heavier while I creep deeper into the darkness and my eyes adjust. The cave walls are complexly contoured with ripples of grooves and spiny outcroppings which almost remind me of the giant urchins of the Boiled Sea. The cold wind continues to blow over me, and I crush my arms across my chest when I shiver.

"You shouldn't have followed me." The little boy shadow's voice echoes in the narrow space.

I can't tell what direction it came from, and I don't see a hint of its form.

"Journeyman was your father?" I ask.

"He was my body's father," the shadow says from the darkness.

I don't really know how to reply to that, not exactly sure what it really means, and I turn slowly, hoping to spot the shadow. Is he there behind that stalagmite? Or is that him tucked into that little alcove, hardly more than a fold in the cave wall?

"Do you know where that woman is taking you?" the shadow asks.

"To find some kid who caused her boss problems. I'm supposed to convince him to come with me and talk to some judge."

"And you're going to do it?"

I shrug.

"I guess? What else can I do? I don't know how else I can get home, and it might help bring some peace to my brother. Or my brother's shadow? Honestly, I feel so lost about everything."

"The nature of this place is to be lost," the shadow says.

He sounds closer, though I can't at all tell from where because of the echoes. Is he in front of me or behind me?

"I just want to go home," I say.

"True home is the place from which you came before your body was born into the World of Light. And I suspect I know the boy of which you speak. If the boy is brought to The Judge, then my father's labor is for nothing, so I'll send you home instead."

A rock clatters. The stone echoes when it tumbles. There's a silence for the length of my inhale, and a plunk when the rock falls into some unseen well below. I try to turn a slow circle, squinting as hard as I can, searching for anything moving. Anything that could be the shape of a person. But the darkness is so thick around me, my eyes just can't make out enough.

Cold breath splashes on the back of my neck. It's not the draft blowing through the cave. The shadow's presence is right behind me. Goosebumps cover my whole body. My skin lights electric with anticipation.

The jagged piece of stone biting into my neck gashes into my esophagus before severing my artery. My eyes roll up when my blood sprays down and out. My body gives way, and the cold rock greets me.

***

You made the wrong decision. The correct choice was to wait for Miela. Turn to page 99.

Somewhere it was said the only thing evil needs to triumph is for good folks to do nothing. Looking at the jagged piece of glass in that little girl's hand and the practically demonic look on her face, I can totally see why evil is probably going to take home the prize. Holy shit, my legs shake when she passes by.

The little girl shadow stops in front of the cart man, the one she called Journeyman, and the shadows watching from atop the rocks grow still. The first little boy shadow creeps forward slowly, his hands opening and closing. His eyes are also locked on Journeyman. His lips press together, and his whole mouth twitches with anger. What could the man have done to these children? Is that why he is supposed to pull the cart, even when his legs are oozing puss everywhere?

The little girl waves the shard of glass under his nose and hisses, "What do you have to say for yourself, Journeyman?"

Journeyman looks down. If there was any color left in his face, it's gone now, but he doesn't seem particularly afraid of the jagged blade.

"Nothing that I didn't already say to The Judge," Journeyman says.

"You left us to Shopkeeper. When Shopkeeper vanished, no one would make a deal with us. They drove us out of Gissu."

Journeyman shrugs.

"Try Synoro or Shilpakala, or any of the towns around the capital. I can't help you anymore," Journeyman says. His eyes fall on the first little boy shadow for a moment before they flit away. "I couldn't even help my son."

The little boy shadow stops his slow advance.

"He never forgave you, you know, after he found out," the little boy shadow says. "It tore him up inside so badly that I ended up here."

Sobs rack the shoulders of Journeyman. Anguish drags his face down like he is starting to melt.

"I just wanted to help him find his way forward," Journeyman bawls. "He was so sick. I would have given anything of myself."

"And us," one of the shadows atop the rocks calls.

"You did it so you would feel like you did something," another shouts. "To hell with what happened to us."

Journeyman falls to his knees between the cart poles and buries his face in his hands. The other shadow children clamber down from the rocks with astonishing agility, and they close in on us in a tightening semicircle. I step nervously toward the cart, unable to picture a kid that small getting the best of me. But there are seven of them, and they sure don't seem to have any fear.

"We heard they'd sent you this way," the little girl shadow whispers. She brings her blade right up to the corner of Journeyman's eye.

He does not flinch away.

"We've been waiting for so long for this chance."

The whole cart groans when Miela steps onto the bench. A moment ago, I practically forgot she existed, and I don't think any of the shadow children even acknowledged her. Now, however, she seems like she's ten feet tall, the way she towers over us all from her perch. The early morning light reflects fiery orange around her.

"Enough of this," she says.

The shadow girl and boy both let their gazes run down Miela's zipper. They look to each other.

"She's an officer of The Court," the boy whispers.

"Yes, and by Libericia's Light, you can cast your judgment on this...man, but you will allow myself and my charge to pass."

The little girl shadow drives her glass blade straight through Journeyman's eye. There's an awful crunch when she rams it through bone and into his brain. His other eye rolls back until it's nothing but white, and his body spasms. His back clenches rigid before all the strength in his body gives way. He collapses to the ground, the impact driving the glass shard in even further.

A single, final exhale leaves his lips, and his figure fades like a movie ghost, leaving nothing but a slight imprint in the pebbles.

"Feel better?" Miela asks.

The little girl shadow shakes her head. She appraises me with a nasty smile. "I suppose I could kill him, and it would be much more permanent, but I don't think I begrudge him anything yet." She pauses and looks to her companions, then back to Miela. "You taking the upper passes to the caldera or heading down to The Daggers?"

Miela considers the question.

Out of the corner of my eye, I watch the little boy shadow slink away from the others. He tosses me a direct glance over his shoulder, like he wants me to follow him. The boy disappears among the rocks, into some sort of dark culvert. Or a cave mouth?

"The caldera to catch the train to Chhoya at the station," she says. "I have no desire to consort with The Foreman or any of his taskmasters."

The little girl nods.

"Then come with me," she says. "We've got a secret path that'll save you a whole day."

Miela grunts.

"And you expect what in return?" she asks.

"Just got a little deal we can make."

The girl's malicious grin grows huge. She gestures off to the side, and Miela follows her off out of earshot. Apprehension squirms in my belly like a parasite. It's hard to imagine they have good things planned for me. Not that any of this has been comforting. I still hardly even know what I'm expected to do.

I turn back to where the little boy disappeared. The other shadows didn't see me notice his departure. This might be a chance for me to get the upper hand and find out some kind of answer for myself.

*****

Follow the little boy shadow and find out if he's up to
something. Turn to page 92.

Wait for Miela. She might not have your best interest at heart,
but she seems expected to be responsible for you.
Turn to page 99.

As discreetly as possible, I inch towards Miela and the little girl shadow. They speak in low whispers, though, so try as I might, I just can't make out what they're saying. Even when I close in on the other shadows half surrounding them, the words escape me until they both reach their hands out and shake.

The first word I understand is the same from both their mouths at once: "Deal."

Miela turns to me.

"We'll leave the cart here and follow them. The girl's name is Witchhazel."

"Just call me Hazel," the little girl adds.

"Apparently," Miela says impatiently, "we can catch a train that will take us all the way to the caldera."

The caldera? Isn't that something to do with volcanos? Not that a volcano in The Shadowlands could be much worse than everything else here, but I don't like this. They stepped away from me to negotiate, which means that whatever deal they made must involve either me doing something or them doing something to me.

Just when I don't think I can hate this place anymore.

"And what do we have to do in return?"

"I'll worry about that," Miela says.

The heat rises in my face, and pressure builds behind my eyes. I'm so tired of this, of the way this place works.

"No, *I'll* worry about that," I say. "Because you're going to tell me to do something horrible. *Or* let these shadows do something horrible to me."

Miela's hands lash out and twist into my shirt so hard, the seams at the shoulders rip partially. She pulls me close to her and jerks the fabric up, holding my balance in her hands.

"My duty is to bring you and the target to The Judge," she says. "You will not say or imply that I will do *anything* but that. Do you understand?"

There is nothing else I can do. "Yes, I understand."

Miela's hands tighten on my shirt, and she shoves me forward toward the road. If there was a point in this trip where I felt like I had the freedom to make choices, this is where it is clear that I do not. I'm a prisoner, no doubt about it.

Hazel pays me no mind. She starts down the road, and we follow. The other kid shadows fall back as we go, lingering a moment to watch before they turn back to wherever they came from to begin with. The little boy shadow follows us a bit further, but before too long, he heads back as well.

Our path winds off the road quickly and takes us through narrow passages among the stones. So much of the spaces I've seen in The Shadowlands are places with skinny paths like these: winding among the urchins, the border town built among the basalt columns, and now this. Is it because the shadows are so much stronger here? It must be only at midday, when the sun is straight overhead, that there is no darkness among paths like these. Maybe the shadows are more at home in the pitch.

The rocks grow larger until we are marching toward a crevasse in a mountainous slope. Ahead, it quickly turns into a tunnel of—I tilt my head back—what looks to be a sizeable mountain. Why didn't I see it when we were approaching? Was I just not looking up? Shouldn't I have seen it from miles away?

Miela steps up beside me and starts to talk. We enter the crevasse, and darkness envelops.

"When The Thirteen broke the world to banish The Eater of Light, it wasn't so simple as throwing their enemy in chains and pushing it into a prison. The Eater of Light wasn't something with a body like you and I or a defined presence like the living shadows. The Eater—like darkness itself—was part of the fabric of reality. The only way to remove darkness from the world is to remove what is lit."

In front of us, Hazel begins to descend. Miela and I come to a staircase leading in a long curve down into the depths of the crevasse.

Miela continues. "There's places in this world that are mistakable for a dim version of the World of Light—huge farms and forests and mountain ranges—but there's also places like this, where the gashes the banishing left still weep like a fresh scar. In such places, one moment you could walk underneath one of those gaps in reality and find everything around you changes as if, in a single step, you'd gone twenty miles."

"Can there just be one normal thing about this place?" I ask.

Miela pauses. She reaches into her pocket, pulls out a mint, and hands it to me.

"Is this going to make me retch like the blackwater did?"

Miela chuckles.

"One day, you'll get the chance to watch someone try blackwater for the first time, and you won't say a damn thing because it's worth the laughter here. But no. That's a mint. It will taste like mint. It's real food from the World of Light, and it's a taste of something you'll find normal in this place."

Part of me wants to be suspicious. To assume she is going to poison me. But I can't possibly think of a reason she would kill me that way, not with all the other choices she surely has.

Besides, there has to be worse ways to go than with minty fresh breath.

Hazel looks back to us. She is fiddling with a wooden crate mounted to the wall. Rusted hinges cry when she raises the lid and pulls out an old, battered lantern and box of matches. It takes three strikes to light the wick, but it makes a good flame when it does. The darkness I didn't even realize settled around us breaks in flickering orange.

"We've got to hurry," she says. "It'll be here any minute."

I pop the mint onto my tongue and suck on it gently. The coolness invades my cheeks and my tongue, and the sweetness feels incredible. It is the best thing I've ever tasted in my life, and I carefully draw air in through my mouth to relish the chill. My belly churns loudly, so loud it echoes around us.

"Sometimes, it's best to let hunger sleep," Miela says.

"Hell with that," I reply. "Holy shit, nothing's ever tasted this good."

Miela smirks on one side of her mouth. She seems genuinely amused.

"Good." And then her smile drops away, and she points ahead of us.

The little girl shadow reaches the bottom of the stairs and disappears through an arched doorway.

"Because in a few minutes, we're going to have to jump onto the roof of a moving train."

I pause. Yup. That sounds about the kind of direction I was expecting this all to head in. It's a really good mint, though, that's for sure.

I keep telling myself that while I step through the archway into a small room. At one end, the structure has collapsed, burying whatever lay that way under a mountain of stone. In the floor, however, someone has broken through and created an opening about a square yard in size. Beneath it, nothing but blackness. Hazel sets the lantern on the ground by the hole.

"Okay," Miela says. "According to the girl, the train runs directly below us. Do you feel it?"

She puts her palms to the ground, and I follow suit. Sure enough, after a few seconds, the vibration comes through the ground. It grows stronger by the moment until it's like I'm standing on top of an earthquake. It reminds me of the thunder before the upward rain, but this time, it's constant, rattling my bones and my teeth.

The roar bursts from underneath us with an explosion of wind. I can't hear anything while Hazel steps around the hole in the ground and jumps through, without so much as a gesture, wave, or nod. Miela pushes me to the edge of the hole.

It's too dark down there to see anything at all. No hint of the train or its speed. Only the roar and the wind from what might as well be an infinite blackness.

I can barely hear when Miela shouts, *"Jump now!"*

*****

Jump now. Turn to page 104.

Holy shit, no. Turn to page 107.

I step up to the opening. My stomach wants to drop right out of my asshole. It's like a hundred live snakes twist in my guts. Who does this? Who jumps into a black hole? Even if it works out, best-case scenario, I'm jumping onto a freaking moving train.

Holy shit. Holy shit.

My breath accelerates into hyperventilation. My heart's a rabbit's foot thumping to warn the colony. If I don't piss myself before I hit bottom, I'll be shocked. But I can't wait any longer. If I don't jump now—

With both feet together and my hands pressed to my side, I hop neatly into the hole.

For a moment, I'm suspended in time. The lantern light around me vanishes.

I strike something. Hard. My legs go out from under me like I'm being sucked sideways into a massive vacuum, and when my shoulder hits something flat, I bounce up into the air. The hole I jumped through is a tiny square of light speeding away from me, leaving me in total darkness before I can blink. Then my body hits again and bounces like I'm a skipping stone thrown across a pond. I go senseless, even when I collide with the train top for the third time. This contact lasts longer.

I'm simply lying on a metal surface shrieking beneath me. Friction drags me closer to the speed of the roaring car.

I'm only gliding when the surface disappears beneath me, and I drop into the gap between cars. The lower half of my body bangs into the metal door of the next car, and my upper body sprawls onto the roof like I'm a ragdoll. All sorts of things jolt in my bones, and awful pains flare in my shoulders and neck. I grasp frantically for something that will keep me from falling into the gap, where I'll be crushed underneath the wheels.

My right hand closes around a metal, vertical pole about the diameter of a quarter. I swing my body. My momentum shifts, and my wrist cries out when it's bent further than it wants to be bent. I manage to catch the doorframe of the opposite car and stop my pivot before it breaks my arm. The vibration of the track beneath rattles my teeth, and I twist to the pole I'm still gripping, taking a hold of a second one parallel to it.

No, not poles. The sides of a ladder. My feet find the rungs, and I lower myself down to the narrow platform meant to provide a step from one car to the other.

I press my back to the car door.

"I'm not dead," I say. "I'm not dead, I'm not dead, I'm not dead."

The door behind me glides open, and I fall backward into someone's arms.

"Not yet," a voice calls into my ears over the air still roaring around us.

It's Tommy.

For a heartbeat, a wave of manic joy surges through me. My brother. I'm in the arms of my brother. He's alive!

When I turn, the darkness of his form becomes clear in the dim glow of lanterns mounted to the walls of the train car. He is curved lines among the more angular shadows thrown from the large, dark crates occupying much of the car's space. Of course, it's Shadow Tommy.

The Shadow Tommy who dragged me here. The one I thought I was trying to help, only for him to ditch me to save his own ass. The one who left me with Miela. The one Miela claims killed actual Tommy.

He's smiling a big, dumbass smile right in front of me.

Anger fills every part of my being.

Did he drown my brother? Did he take his head and hold him under? Or drag him down by the legs? Club him senseless and roll him over the edge?

Supposedly, Tommy is the one who made bad deals or something, and maybe that's part of how I ended up here, but none of that matters right now. This shadow—this one right in front of me—becomes the target of everything bad I have felt since my brother's funeral.

Hell. Since *before* Tommy's funeral.

He extends his arms to give me a great big hug.

*****

Hug him. Turn to page 112.

Throw him under the train. Turn to page 114.

So, the thing is, that there's just some lines that aren't meant to be crossed. Some decisions you don't make. You don't stick your arm into an industrial meat grinder. You don't poke your hand into a sink garbage disposal. You don't put cyanide in your mouth to see if it really does taste like almonds. You don't jump through a tiny hole into pitch blackness, hoping you'll land on a moving train.

Unfortunately, as perfectly reasonable as all these things are, there is an underlying and inescapable truth in situations where you are forced to contemplate such questions: If you don't jump through, then you get pushed.

"Go," Miela bellows. Her hands shove me hard between the shoulder blades.

I stumble forward too fast, and my hips smack against the far side of the hole while my legs disappear inside. The wind rushing against my calves is hurricane force, and my hands scrabble for purchase but fail to find it. My weight drags me down, my chest scraping against the edge of the opening.

I frantically jerk my arms about for *anything* to hold onto. My elbow strikes the lantern. It tips over, and the glass bubble shatters on the rock. The fuel can built into its base splashes its contents across the flame, and the burning liquid splashes all over my back. The room bursts glaringly bright.

I'm through the hole, falling at a weird angle, heat blooming all around me and searing the entirety of my back. My high-pitched shriek cuts off just as it begins, when my feet collide with something moving at an absurd speed. Friction pulls my legs out from under me, and I pitch forward. My chest and hands hit curved metal, and I try to grab onto it when my momentum goes sideways.

I roll over the edge of the train roof, grasping for a hold that will let me stop my weight. The howling wind keeps the fire from burning as fiercely as it would have, but it doesn't fully extinguish it. I'm shrieking again when the burns bite deeper into my muscles. My body enters the open air beside the train.

For another instant, I'm falling, but my foot snags on something protruding from the side of the train. My hands lurch down over my head, and one of them strikes something hard and unyielding. The pain explodes before the crunch, so loud it reaches my ears over the sound of the train and the rushing wind. My body rebounds and snaps straight. My arms wave up and back down. I catch a glimpse of the stump of my wrist and the splintered bones of my forearm shining with blood in the light of the flames roasting me alive.

When my other hand hits the ground, the agony is equal, but this time, the appendage pulverizes in a burst of red mist and dark chunks. The blow is so fast, it's like my hand is there and then it isn't, but then my mind processes the flight of some of the pieces.

Not that it matters.

Burning fuel has spread over more of my body, and flames lick at my eyes, even as the blow twists my spine so my uncaught leg swings out sideways and strikes something itself. The pain explodes from toes to knee. My leg might as well have never existed from the midpoint of my femur down. Nonetheless, part of the space that was my leg is outlined by incomprehensible pain.

The dizziness hits when my blood drains out of the wounds I haven't fully processed.

My leg comes free from where it is caught because of all the torque of being banged around. I'm pretty sure the leg itself is the thing that broke. When I hit the ground, my remaining leg crashes down, and there's a sudden pressure across my pelvis unlike anything I've ever felt.

Oh my god, I've been run over. The flames on my torso flare when oil sprays from the wheels. My eyes sizzle, boiling in their sockets. I tumble against the wall of the tunnel and strike my head, but it's okay because everything goes black.

***

You chose wrong. The correct answer was Jump Now.
Turn to page 104.

And it's a long kiss, like they don't give a shit that I'm there. Like I'm totally inconsequential. Like it doesn't matter that they put on a whole dog and pony show for me.

Tommy's shadow never ditched me for her. He turned me over to her in a way that left me stranded. If all that was a performance, can I trust anything they said? Did Tommy sell out Shadow Tommy? Did Shadow Tommy kill Tommy? Hell, did I just suffer a psychotic break and am not really here to begin with?

I clench my fists. That's it. I've had it.

What will being run over by a train do to either of them? Shadow Tommy said it wouldn't kill him, but I've seen enough slasher movies to know that even if the killer does keep on coming, there's some serious satisfaction to be had in watching the victim fight back.

As for Miela, she has a body. It may be a zip-up body—whatever the hell that really implies—but it's a body, nonetheless. Will she die like I supposedly would, or will it just send her back to the World of Light like it did Journeyman? How the hell am I supposed to make decisions in a world with a parallel set of laws of physics? The thing which really matters, though, is Journeyman suffered when those scorpions stung him. And it hurt him when Hazel sent him back for sure.

Who knows, maybe having her chest crushed will crush that void and the scales inside it into nothing.

I plant my foot and lunge forward while the two kiss. One step, two steps, three steps. I curl my arm to my body and thrust my shoulder out like a linebacker, ramming into them with all my weight. Together, they launch backward, still clinging to each other, their feet off the ground, sailing toward the open door.

Miela's hands sweep from Shadow Tommy's shoulders. Her fingers stay clenched around the weapons, and her hands slam into the doorframe. The door bangs against the wall with a loud crack when Tommy's weight crashes into her.

For a split second, I hope his weight will drive her through, but the absolute fury etched into Miela's snarl will give me no such luck. With a roar, she jerks her body forward against Shadow Tommy and sends him staggering toward me, even as my own momentum makes me stumble another step. We collide at the shoulder, and I twist to the side, slamming into the same door. Hard splinters buckle up from its center.

The air rushes out of me in a powerful *woof*. Miela steps fully back into the car and right up to me. Both her hands clench together, and before I can move, she jerks them above her right shoulder and drives them forward.

I try to close my mouth against the blow, but she's still holding those knives.

Both blades punch through my teeth and gums, jerking to a stop when they grind my upper and lower jaw bones. The violation of my face erupts in agony. I can only manage an *urk* sound because Miela drags the blades down simultaneously with all her strength.

They sheer through my lower jaw and my esophagus. Any hope of a scream ends when she decimates my vocal cords. The crunch as she breaks through my sternum is unlike anything I've ever heard, like a thousand knuckles cracking inside me.

Those blades must be so sharp. Driven with such force. The arc of her movement glides them through my diaphragm, severing my organs and all the sinew, until the blades sweep out just below my navel.

I can't make a sound. My blood and viscera sluice through the massive channel she opened in me.

The last thing I see is the smirk spreading on Miela's face.

The last thing I hear is her say, "If you had a zipper, you'd be just like me now."

***

Wrong choice. Try again. Turn to page 116.

I try to hold the anger in. But after crossing a chunk of The Shadowlands with Journeyman and the Zip Up Lady, then nearly dying from landing on top of a speeding train, holy hell, it's nice to see someone who reminds me of my normal life, even if he's just a shadow of it. I throw my arms around him and tell myself it's Tommy.

It's Tommy. It's Tommy.

We stand there in the train car's flickering light, among boxes and crates bound for who knows where.

And it's Tommy.

There are some moments in life where time seems to stop. One was the moment I jumped into a dark hole onto a speeding train. Another was this. And unlike jumping to my likely death but not letting myself think on it too much, this moment is different. This is one of healing.

In this moment, I try to pass on all my "I love yous" and "Goodbyes" and "I'd take it back if I coulds" to my brother through his shadow, as if it is some sort of conduit. If love is a real force, I try so hard to channel it now, to conjure it to The Shadowlands and pull my brother back into a living world, even if it's this dark place.

If we were here together, I know we could find a way to be free from Miela, Hazel, and whatever little boy I'm supposed to con into meeting with the mysterious judge. There is no way something good will come of that; I feel it in my bones.

Something inside Shadow Tommy is cold enough that the chill of his body through his clothes presses through mine, and something warm in my heart cools too. I step back and set my hands on Shadow Tommy's shoulders, giving him a squeeze.

"My brother's dead," I say. It's not a question or an argument. It's just words coming out of my mouth that I know to be true.

"Sometimes, things in life just don't work out." Shadow Tommy looks down at his feet, at mine. His eyes look anywhere on the ground and the walls but at me. "Or they work out, but just not the way you thought they would, and then you understand you never really knew what you were doing in the first place."

"I took him so for granted," I say.

Shadow Tommy nods solemnly. He places his hands on my shoulders and squeezes me back.

"You took everything for granted," he says.

I cock my head at him.

"What do you mean?"

But there's a sorrow in his eyes, a regret, which sends lightning up my spine. Something is wrong.

I open my mouth to ask him what's going on, but I suspect Miela is standing right behind me. Even though she's not especially big—because I can't see her—she feels ten feet tall. If I look up, there will be her eyes looking down, maybe her chest unzipped and tentacles streaming out of the darkness inside her.

She releases a long, slow breath through her nose. It reminds me of when she meant to let Journeyman die. She will hurt me no matter what I do. There's a *woosh* of air, and I can't even react before her thumbs jam into my eyes.

It's a strange feeling to have my eyes crushed. For blunt objects like fingers to shove my corneas through the vitreous humor and into the back of my sockets, crushing them through my retinas and into my optic nerves. I register the utter intrusion for a millisecond.

When the lights go out, the agony explodes. My bladder and bowels both release, and my body gives a tremendous shudder.

***

Wrong choice. The correct choice was to throw him under the train. Turn to page 114.

I slam the flat of my fist against the wall of the train. Something in the cheap, papered veneer cracks, and I grind my teeth at the sudden pain in my hand.

"Are you kidding?" I say. "If you'd just left me home, I'd be with my parents. We'd have left the funeral and gone to eat with the rest of the family. I'd hear everyone muttering about me, and they'd all stare daggers through me. It would have sucked, and Mom and Dad would have treated me like a stone around their necks, but then we'd have gone home. Maybe I'd have killed some time playing video games or watching TV and just been able to stew. I'd have gotten ready for bed and fallen asleep in a damn *bed*. I slept last night in a wooden cart in the middle of a field, where it rains up and where these asshole little shadow scorpions come crawling out of the damn rocks in swarms."

I take a step forward and point my index finger right in Shadow Tommy's face. He flinches. Dark beads of shadow sweat shimmer on his forehead. He takes a small retreating step, trying to look behind him to make sure he isn't about to bump into one of the aisle seat backs.

"'Get in the coffin,' you said," I snap. "'Trust me,' you said. Or whatever the hell it was you said that talked me into coming to this insane place. The only question I've had since I've been here—aside from the thousands of questions that are so insane that I shouldn't even have to consider them—is why am I not dead?"

I slap my palms onto Shadow Tommy's shoulders.

"But you know what? At this point, what I want to know is why I shouldn't kill you."

Shadow Tommy knits his brows. He gives me the dumbest smirk I've ever seen.

"Because it won't kill me?" he says.

"Oh yeah?"

I grab the fabric of his shirt, plant my feet, and pivot hard. The shadow's weight lurches with the force, and I ram my hip against him when he falls away from me. The blow sends him staggering into the doorway to the space between the cars.

Miela drops down from the train roof into the doorway and shoves Shadow Tommy at me. He collides with me hard, and we both stagger backward. My foot catches on something, and I fall onto my ass. His butt crashes down right where my belly meets my ribs, and the wind rushes out my lungs. My diaphragm spasms. I gasp so hard, it's also a groan.

"Now, boys, that's no way to settle a dispute." Miela pulls her zipper halfway down her chest. With her left hand, she reaches in and draws out a shining silver bowie knife. With her right, she retrieves a dagger with a blade as black as anything I've ever seen. Deeper than onyx. Like light has never touched it. "You need something more like these for this kind of work."

She admires both blades in turn and then points them toward us. Her arms move with a lithe grace, but there is tension in them. They're each like coiled snakes waiting to strike. She focuses in on Shadow Tommy.

"I didn't think I'd be seeing you so soon."

"What can I say?" Shadow Tommy eyes the blades in Miela's hands. He seems especially cautious about the black one. "I've got business to conclude."

Miela takes a step closer and smirks. "And here I was, hoping you were just the type to break a deal."

"Glad to disappoint," Shadow Tommy says, smirking too.

He steps closer to her as well.

Wait a damn minute. They're making eyes at each other. Shadow Tommy reaches forward and zips Miela back up to her neck.

"Well, you do that a lot," Miela says. "So I'm glad you make the most of it."

And then his hands land on her hips, and she rests her wrists on his shoulders, still holding her blades. They lean against each other and kiss.

*****

Throw them under the train. Turn to page 110.

What the hell? Turn to page 117.

Run. Turn to page 120.

What else is there for me to say but, 'What the hell?'

I mean really, what the hell?

Am I staring daggers at them? If they stop freaking kissing, are they going to look at me and see how much shade I'm throwing? Because with those actual daggers in her hands, nasty squints are about my only recourse. Especially since heading out the door they're blocking puts me in reach of those blades. Behind me, the car's main floor is choked with crates and boxes, and I don't even know if I would be able to get to the door on the far side.

They finally spread apart, and even then, they take several seconds to turn to me.

Shadow Tommy shrugs and holds his hands palms-up.

"Surprise?" he says.

"Seriously, why? Why all the lying? Was this all a game for you? Because I'm pretty sure I've been one step away from death every moment of the last twenty-four hours."

"Nah, man, you got it all wrong," Shadow Tommy says. "We've got a really simple job. To bring you to your destination. No more, no less, no bullshit, no lies. This was just the only way to get you through."

"You couldn't have told me—" But then I stop. "Wait. Did Tommy know?"

Miela and Shadow Tommy look at each other. They burst out laughing.

"Holy shit, that would be awkward." Shadow Tommy snickers.

"Yeah, man, I'm just gonna crouch down and make out with your shadow." Miela chuckles back before forcing herself composed. She holds a playful finger to Tommy's lips. "To be fair, though, I'm the one who told Tommy about The Shadowlands. I brought him over for the first time. He wouldn't have ever met his shadow."

"That turned out well for him," I say.

"It might have, if you'd cared enough to keep an eye on him," Miela responds.

That hurts, but this isn't anything I can solve. Something still doesn't add up about this.

"So, wait," I say. "You took him to The Shadowlands. You had to have led him through, like you've led me through, because the kinds of deals you claim he made wouldn't have been done in the good part of town. And with all that, you let him sell out his own shadow for favors?"

Miela's face grows hard. She steps toward me. The daggers in her hands coil back. She could lash out at any time, and I doubt I could block it.

"You know, for someone who is supposed to be an apathetic nothing, you care way too much about this."

I shuffle slowly backward, feeling the area behind myself. My hand brushes against a crate, and I adjust my path, with the hopes I don't back into a corner. Miela continues to advance. I try to glance side to side, but I can't do it far enough to see a way without taking my eyes off Miela. If that happens, I'm pretty sure it's just a blink and I'm done.

"We could tell him," Shadow Tommy says.

"Tell me what?"

My heel bangs against another crate, and my breath catches.

"No." Miela's face is a smug mask. "We're not movie villains. Besides, we're close enough to The Judge that we can do this with just his corpse."

She lunges, bringing both daggers together at my neck from opposite directions, severing my arteries and my throat. I gag when gluts of blood pump into the air, and an explosion of blackness overwhelms me.

***

Wrong choice. Try again. Turn to page 116.

I grit my teeth and clench the dagger. Whatever is coming, I'm going to take it down. I can do this. Because I've made it this far, this will be easy.

The reverberation of the blow striking the door rattles my whole skeleton. My teeth clack so hard, I'm shocked I don't have a mouth full of enamel shards. The door itself is massively concaved inward, and a fissure in the metal has opened from the corner to the midpoint. In the darkness through the tear, a massive shape looms.

I don't get a good look at it, other than a gaping mouth from which dozens of needle-sharp teeth jut. Maybe it is just my mind. There is no way something with all those teeth is not a figment of my imagination.

*****

Nope. Go to I can't stop now. I can't! Turn to page 137.

Nuh uh. Go to I can't stop now. I can't! Turn to page 137.

I turn to bolt. The car is littered with crates, and there's no clear path—at least not one that doesn't involve me climbing somewhere. Oh hell, I hope that's thick enough wood to hold my weight.

I launch toward what looks like the path of least resistance. It's a five-step sprint before I shove myself up onto a four-foot box, and at the top, I'm ready to slide down the other side when I freeze. The ground below is covered in some sort of black substance. It reminds me of the face of the border guard who made a copy of my head.

With my eyes, I follow the pool to a broken crate. It's a smaller box, but its sides have collapsed outward, and shards of some sort of ceramic jar lie about around it. I don't like the looks of it. To me, it screams "Do Not Touch," but the only other way through seems like it's going to be to climb on top of the crates next to me.

They're slightly smaller, maybe three feet high, and they also look thinner. When I test the crate I'm on by shifting my weight a little, the wood planks flex underneath my heels like cheap plywood. That's a recipe for neck breaking right there.

Two throats clear behind me. Miela and Shadow Tommy stand with their arms crossed and their heads tilted, like they're looking at a confusing painting. If I were a painting, I guess I'd be "Man on Crate?" Regardless, I'm not very good at running, I guess.

"Do we need to call the fire department to help you down?" Miela asks.

"I hear that shadow cats get themselves stuck in trees sometimes," Shadow Tommy adds. "You think he's part shadow cat?"

"What say we take his pelt?" Miela tilts her dagger.

"I don't think The Judge would like that."

Miela shrugs.

"We're close enough that his shadow will still be clinging to his corpse when we get there," she says.

My shadow clinging to my corpse?

There's no time to think about it. I look back to the black pool and up the crate stack.

*****

Jump over the pool. I can make it. Turn to page 122.

Climb up the crates. They won't break. Turn to page 124.

I take one last glance at the crates. My best bet is to try to clear the black pool. It's not that far across the gap, and I'm already a few feet up. I made bigger jumps at the playground as a kid. It would be easier if I could get a running start, but that would put me in the reach of Miela and Shadow Tommy. Instead, I give my arms a quick swing back. My knees bend, my butt drops low, and I tilt just a little. I thrust my arms forward and straighten my legs as hard as I can, pushing off the crate edge.

The crate fractures under the pressure with a gunshot crack, and the plank breaks backward, absorbing my momentum with the shift in force. Instead of launching out, my body straightens in place. My feet fall inside the crate through the newly formed gap, catching on the edge. My upper body arcs downward, and I turn my outstretched arms to break my fall.

My palms slap straight into the black goo, and my left wrist erupts in a volcano of pain with a second crack. My hand slides sideways more than an inch, in a way it was never meant to, the instant before my chin crashes into the pool and against the steel floor underneath. When my molars shatter and my incisors break, it's like I'm crunching hard onto ice from the bottom of a soda, except for the jolts of exposed nerves following the eruption of blood in my mouth.

I spit out a mouthful of tooth, crimson, and about an inch of my lower lip my bottom teeth punched straight through to clear my airway enough to scream. The goo is like the surface of a tarpit or something, and I'm stuck. It's hot too.

I mean, *really* hot.

The pain in my wrist and mouth must have gated it off initially, but the scent of burning flesh invades my nostrils. The surface of the black goo bubbles around my hand. They pop along my chin, and the searing soars into a new crescendo. It creeps up to my cheeks and to my wrists from my arms. Soon both my lower arms and the bottom half of my face are nothing but an internal inferno. The steam rising from my cheeks scalds my nose and eyes.

Light flares around me when my clothes catch fire. All I feel is burning anyway, and all my attempts to scream are nothing more than sputtering whines.

***

Wrong choice. You should have chosen Climb up the crates. They won't break. Turn to page 124.

I cast one last glance at the black goo. It's not that the distance looks too far, but something about the substance simply makes me not want to risk it. An acrid smell in the air, which can only be coming from it, leaves me a little uneasy. I don't know what it'll do if I touch it, and I don't have time to weigh it further. Instead, I grab the edge of the crate on the stack beside me and pull myself up onto it.

Shadow Tommy crawls onto the crate I just left, and Miela is sidling toward the edge of the car, surely attempting to find a path around the blockage.

The crate groans under me, so I spread my weight as much as I can toward the corners. The wood itself feels weirdly spongy, like it's both a little softer than wood should be and is soaking wet. I swallow hard and clamber onto the adjacent crate. If this holds my weight for just a couple more seconds, I'll be over the other side and climbing down toward freedom.

As much freedom as is possible on a speeding train anyways.

With a grunt, I inch forward as fast as I can. My back brushes the roof of the car, and Shadow Tommy is right behind me. He grabs for my foot, but his fingers slip off the toe of my shoe. I swing my legs over the other side and lower them to the crate below.

The whole pile shudders. Something crushes eight feet below me, at whatever point supports the most weight. I clench the sides of the crate I'm on, and while I do so, I look back at Shadow Tommy, where he clings, pressed against the ceiling like I was. His eyes are wide and his body tense.

The crate beneath me collapses, and the sides buckle outward. The crate crashes to the floor of the car, right into the middle of the black pool, but the momentum hurls me off sideways, and I tumble onto the far side. I roll hard against another crate and smash through it. A massive splinter from it jams right up into my ribs. I arch my back and shriek like a baby.

The sole of my shoe brushes the edge of the pool, and the way the goo latches onto it stops my scream in its tracks.

Adrenaline surges when smoke rises almost instantly, and I jerk my foot against the pull. That black crap is climbing up onto my shoe, even while the remains of the crate I rode down smolder and flicker with flames.

The goo does not relinquish its hold, however. It's climbing the sides of my shoe, and it crushes against my foot like a vise grip. I jerk my leg again until it slides right out of my shoe.

When I spill over sideways, the jagged splinter of wood is driven another inch deeper into me. How it has not punctured my lung is a miracle, but I scream again and twist.

Shadow Tommy is at the car's edge, shielding himself from the growing flames among the crates. He must have fallen the other way, against the side of the car.

The side of the car...

Where is Miela?

I grit my teeth so hard I think they'll break and shove myself to my feet despite the pain in my side. Miela is right in front of me when I turn to the back door. She still holds both daggers, and her face is a mask of fury. She swings her arms up and out to plunge her blades into me.

*****

Grab her wrists and drive her own weapons down into her chest. Turn to page 126.

Rip the wooden wedge out of my side and stab her in the throat. Turn to page 128.

Despite the pain in my side, I step towards her and thrust my hands up. Before she can bring the blades down, I catch her at the wrists. I envision the way I need to bend them. The torque I need to apply with my shoulders. The arc the blades will follow so each one plunges into her chest, just above the opposite breast.

It's so clear. A simple sequence of physical motions.

Except the wound in my side, where the splinter of the crate buried into me, is agony.

And she's freakishly strong. I can hold her arms up only because my elbows are locked, but my muscles already start to shake from the force she's bearing down with on my hands.

"I warned Tommy you were more trouble than this whole thing was worth," she says.

My feet slide on the metal floor. I scoot them slightly wider for better balance, but doing so gives her more leverage. The pressure increases when her angle grows more direct. The muscles around my wounded ribs shriek and shudder. My thigh fibers burn. I hated squats in gym, and now I despise straining my thighs to hold myself up.

"This whole thing would have been easier if we could have just killed you at the start," she says.

My blood runs like ice. There's nothing human in her eyes. The heat from my effort clashes against a cold sweat breaking out on my forehead and the middle of my back.

My body shakes like I'm convulsing. I can't hold her up any longer.

A voice whispers in my ear.

"I know what you're thinking," Shadow Tommy says. "But you would have such an easier time understanding if you could just grasp that a person and their shadow are not the same being. And shadows like me and people like Miela, we gotta make our way in this world somehow."

Shadow Tommy lashes out with his hands between my arms and chops me right inside both my elbows. They buckle, and the blades drive straight down. The silver one enters my shoulder right behind my collarbone, and the black blade breaks straight through my sternum.

The air rushes out of me in a soft *herk*. A shudder runs through everything inside me. My eyes are so wide, like they're going to roll out of my skull. My bladder empties. My body tries to collapse, but Miela holds me up by the blades. She pulls my face right up to hers, and the knives grind agonizingly against my bones. Blood gushes down my chest.

A softness floods Miela's face. Her lips smile sweetly, and her eyes deepen with a clear sadness.

She gives me a soft kiss on the cheek. Her breath smells sour.

With a wrenching twist, she jerks both daggers out of me, and I fall to the floor in an instant. My consciousness drains with the blood from my ruptured heart.

***

Wrong choice. You should have chosen Rip the wooden wedge
out of my side and stab her in the throat.
Turn to page 128.

My impulse is to grab her arms and block those blades, but the pain in my side tells me I won't be stopping much of anything. Instead, before I can imagine how much it is going to hurt, I rip out the fat splinter with both hands and thrust it upward.

It pierces Miela's throat just above the top of her zipper and continues into her skull, where it wrenches to a stop. Miela's eyes widen. One of them rolls back, and the other spasms to the side. Her mouth opens, and her throat makes an *ah-ah-ah* sound. The muscles all over her face tremble, as do her arms and torso. Her tendons stand out against her flesh while her body tries to complete its last instruction but fails.

"No!" Shadow Tommy is right behind me, a shining, silver blade I didn't see him draw falling from his fingers. He shoves me aside.

The splinter wrenches out of Miela's throat, pulled by my weight, and a glut of blood bursts in its wake. Tommy catches the collapsing form of the woman in his arms. The daggers she was holding clatter uselessly to the floor right next to his own, and his hand finds her cheek, shadow-black against her pale tone. She is already dead, her eyes open and locked in the dislocation. Her face is one of a broken doll.

"No, no, no," Shadow Tommy bawls. "Disappear. Please. Just disappear."

I remember Journeyman. How he vanished when he was killed. Miela's body looks like an empty vessel of muscle and skin.

"We were going to be free," Shadow Tommy says. "We were finally going to be free."

He rocks back and forth, drawing her tightly to his chest. In the dark blur of his features, glistening tears run. Does he cry blackwater? He tilts his head toward me. In a blink, his face transforms from a mask of anguish to one of rage.

"You did this," he snarls.

When he lets go of Miela's body, she rolls away, limp, and thumps to the floor of the train car. The zipper on her chest has withered, warped and curled, and her mouth hangs open, her tongue slightly out.

Shadow Tommy grabs the two silver blades and rises to his feet.

"We worked so hard so that we could have everything. They were going to let her stay. She was going to stay forever."

"Looks like they kept their word." I point to her body. "They're keeping their deal to the letter."

"Well, I know for sure about you," Shadow Tommy says. "They say dead will be dead."

I want to tell him I know The Shadower wants me to arrive in one piece, but that won't matter to him with Miela gone. He moves forward, waving the daggers with a controlled flourish. I press my hand to my injured side and back up. The pool of black goo is just a couple of steps behind me, and the pain in my side is nearly unbearable.

Right behind him lies the onyx-bladed knife on the floor.

I want to dive, but my wound hurts so bad. He would simply swipe down into my back. However, what if that blade is black for a reason? In the flickering light, it almost seems to glimmer.

What if it's only meant to hurt shadows? Would it hurt me too?

I jerk back to avoid a half-slash from Shadow Tommy's left hand. He might not be the same as Tommy, but surely, they've lived their lives in parallel. The things Tommy saw, so did Shadow Tommy. Some of these memories might mean something to him.

*****

Talk him down. Turn to page 130.

Get the dark blade. Turn to page 135.

I take a step back. My heel lands an inch from the black pool. There's no more room for retreat, but the blood oozing from my side despite the pressure I'm putting on it tells me I don't have another fight in me. This ends with him putting those blades down or my guts on the floor.

I am about to bring up the bus stop, but after what I just learned about him and Miela. I blurt out the first thing that comes to mind. The first memory where I felt like I tried to protect Tommy, as an older brother should.

"Remember Tommy's first day of school?"

Shadow Tommy draws one of his blades back to strike. But he doesn't. His brow furrows. A knit appears between his eyebrows. The smirk drops to a frown.

"A miserable day in a miserable life," Shadow Tommy says.

"But I bet you remember Kaylee, don't you? She was cute, and she liked Tommy."

"And she said it in front of everybody." Shadow Tommy stomps his foot like a little kid.

For a moment, I'm struck by something. All this time, I kind of saw Shadow Tommy as something of an authority on The Shadowlands, but he's still a kid. A kid who thought he found a girl who liked him.

"Tommy got bullied for weeks because of that. He was so embarrassed. Funny how a bunch of dimwit kids chanting about k-i-s-s-i-n-g can leave a mark."

"I remember when Tommy sat next to me on the bus that day," I say. "He was trying so hard not to cry. He told me every name he'd been called. There were so many, I couldn't believe he remembered them all."

Shadow Tommy shrugs.

"He made up a few to keep you listening."

"I still saw how he felt. I still knew that the other kids were just jealous."

The shadow drops his gaze to his feet. He scratches at the back of his head with the handle of his knife. Shadow Tommy looks even more childish now, so much more like the kid who drowned in my parents' pool. Who was buried the day I was brought to The Shadowlands. I can almost think he *is* Tommy.

Without raising his chin, he says softly, "I was jealous too." He takes a long, deep breath and releases it. "That day wasn't the day I decided I wanted to be free of Tommy, but it was one of many moments I thought of when I did. He just wanted to retreat after that. Was always so scared to put him—to put *us*—forward because he just knew he'd be taunted. I tried to whisper at the back of his mind that he couldn't keep on like that, tried to get him to be a body worth being cast from."

He lifts his head and meets my eyes with a hard, cold look.

"This was supposed to be my chance to put myself forward."

He slashes one of the daggers toward Miela and points.

"She was going to be *my* Kaylee." Shadow Tommy's tone gets sharper with each word. "She was my chance to live a life that Tommy would have wanted. That I watched him fail to get."

I swallow.

"Maybe that wasn't the best memory," I say. "There was this time when you got off the bus—"

Shadow Tommy roars and lunges forward, both daggers thrusting at my torso. There is nowhere for me to retreat. To step back is to burn. To stand is to die. I close my eyes and await the pain of being pierced.

It does not come.

Something thuds, and I open my eyes. Shadow Tommy is crumpled in front of me on the floor of the train car. Hazel stands over his body with the black blade in her hand. Blood pulses out of the severed arteries in Shadow Tommy's neck. It's black as night and pooling all about him.

"You killed him," I whisper.

"He was as good as dead," Hazel says. "And you're a lot less deader than you would have been if I hadn't."

Looking at his body is a strange feeling. He's my brother's shadow, but he's also my brother. I can't fully separate the two, no matter how much I try. Tears brim my eyes, and a sob catches in my throat.

"It's okay to be sad," Hazel says. "The Shadowlands is the home of much sadness."

She takes my hand and pulls me toward the door, but I shake my head. I can't leave Tommy just yet. I left his funeral; I can't leave this. Now I need to stand vigil. To tell someone what happened. Hazel accepts my resistance and lets go.

I shiver.

"It's getting really cold," I say.

"That's just the blood loss talking."

"I wish I understood what this was all really about. I just don't get this place. I know you wanted to be free and that you felt you could be free here, but why did you have to bring me into it? Why'd Tommy have to die?"

"I don't really know," Hazel says. "They killed your brother because it's the easiest way to sever a shadow before the body is ready to let it go, but as far as why you're here..."

"Why are *you* here?" I say. No one here has had my best interests at heart, so I don't see why I should expect that from Hazel.

"The boy...a kid named Little Bit...they want you to bring him to The Judge. He brought my whole world down. It's not his fault really. He came here because his shadow was stolen. But when he met Journeyman, the things the kid did in The Shadowlands cost me the living we made dealing with Journeyman and the protection we got from a shadow named Shopkeeper. Our companion Quiet was sentenced to the work lines in the obsidian mines. We were all forced to leave our home and make our way as best we could on the road. People don't cross The Shadower and win. It doesn't happen, and apparently, if it does, bad things happen."

I sigh.

"So, you're going to make me take the kid to The Judge too?"

Hazel shakes her head and sets the shadow dagger beside Shadow Tommy's body.

"I just want to know what the kid has to say for himself. I hope to never, ever meet The Judge again in my life."

"Who is this Judge?" I ask.

"*The* Judge enforces Shadow Law. He doesn't exactly work for The Shadower, but let's just say that their aims are aligned with each other. A lot of shadows will tell you he's the scariest thing in The Shadowlands."

My body shifts a moment, and I stumble slightly. A metallic groan sounds around me, like all the metal in the car is bending at once. The floor beneath my feet shudders roughly and then settles into a loud vibration. We're slowing down. The train is stopping.

Hazel presses her fingers to my elbow. It's the kindest touch I've received the whole time I've been in The Shadowlands, yet it also reminds me of how hurt I really am. My shirt clings to my side, soaked in blood. The wound isn't oozing at the moment, but if I move wrong, it'll split it right open.

"You can still run for it," Hazel says. "You don't even need to see the boy at the train station."

"I have nowhere to go."

"Go home," Hazel says simply.

"I can't."

"Sure, you can. It's easy. I can just kill you like Journeyman."

I shake my head.

"I don't think that that'll work. I'm pretty sure that dead is going to be dead."

Hazel opens her mouth to say something but stops. She looks at me a long moment while the train continues to slow. Her eyes start at my head and drop down to my side. To my waist. To my legs. To the ground around me. Her eyes widen.

"Oh my god," she says.

"What do you mean? What's wrong?"

"This isn't about Little Bit at all. Oh my god."

A tremendous bang sounds from the far end of the car. I turn. Across the puddle of black fluid, past the crates, the door stands closed. A massive dent has buckled it inward.

"What's happening?" I ask, but Hazel is already disappearing through the door between cars behind me.

I want to follow, but the thought of moving kills me. My chest wound throbs just thinking about it. Maybe I can defend this spot against whatever is coming. That black pool is between me and the other door, and I can use that to my advantage.

*****

Stand my ground. Turn to page 119.

"Hazel, wait up!" Turn to page 137.

I step back until my heel is right at the edge of the black goo. Any further, and I'll go up in flames. Already, the air is filled with the stinging stink of smoke and acrid fumes. My eyes water and my vision blurs. I bend my knees and tense, ready to dive for the blade. He sees the flex and adjusts his stance accordingly. If I can get past him, it's going to be by the skin of my teeth.

"You know, when I first stumbled into The Shadowlands, Tommy had fallen asleep in the music room at school," Shadow Tommy says. "He'd been so scared of getting on the bus that day that he'd hidden out until all the buses were gone, and then he convinced his teachers to drive him home."

"I remember. When I saw him get out of that car, it was late. Right before Mom was supposed to get home. He made me swear not to tell Mom and Dad."

"Remember what you did?"

I nod slowly.

"I was worried about you. Worried that something was wrong that I couldn't fix."

"And they told the principal, and the school made sure I was on the bus every day after."

"There was the day at the bus stop—"

"Almost two years of me being pushed around and spit on before that. When you left my school—"

"You could have told the school."

"Nothing they could do," Shadow Tommy says. "But the thing is, it didn't matter. By the time you 'saved me' at the bus stop, it didn't matter." He rolls his wrists, and his fingers clench harder on the daggers. "Tommy needed to be protected, but I was done. I was trading umbrellas and old shoes at Shade Row. I took a boat down the Shadowrun. Me. Just me. No scared little Tommy to hold me back.

"Do you know how much I hated Tommy because his body always pulled me back to him when he woke? Here, there was no big brother Danny to be my crutch. When Miela met Tommy, she was a revelation. A goddess. I slipped away from Tommy in his sleep and found her in The Shadowlands. Do you know that she hunted shadow wolves? That she'd managed to work her way into the presence of The Shadower himself?"

He looks to the side like he expects The Shadower to be standing beside us so he can point to him and say, "Right there. He's right there."

I won't get a better chance, so I lurch into a dive and sail toward the weapon.

His knee drops, and his fist comes down like a hammer, driving the blade right between my shoulders. Bone deflects the knife through my right lung, and it twists and jerks between my ribs. Something crunches inside me. I try to scream, but he pulls the blade out right before I make any sound, and the air won't come. My diaphragm spasms desperately, and my mouth opens and closes at the air, like a fish out of water.

"I'm going to pay an awful price for this," Shadow Tommy says into my ear, "but if she's gone, it's worth it to know that I'll stand on my own for a few short hours before I do."

He rises and walks out the car door, shutting me in. The darkness in my eyes closes in too.

***

Wrong choice. You should have chosen Talk him down.
Turn to page 130.

I limp after Hazel as fast as I can. Not only has the train slowed, but flickering torches are mounted at regular intervals on the tunnel wall. The train jolts over something in the tracks, and I brace myself by grabbing the ladder before I step across the gap. When I do so, my eyes drop into the space between cars, and I notice a long wavering thing, almost like a cross section of the body of a massive snake. It stretches from beneath the car I'm entering to beneath the one I just left.

Some sort of massive shadow serpent maybe?

I swing across the gap, trying to keep my other hand pressed to the wound in my side, controlling how much the motion pulls on the injury. A fresh peal of pain rocks me like thunder.

"Gah!" I bang against the doorway instead, tumbling on in and limping deeper into the car. It's another storage car like the other, but this one is far more organized, with crates neatly stacked and tied down on either side.

A crash so loud it jolts my bones sounds behind me. The car I'm in lurches forward. Things grind, bang, and smash. A chanced glance tells me all I need to know.

The train decoupled behind me.

Sparks explode around wheels grinding metal an instant before the car with Shadow Tommy and Miela's bodies pivots ninety degrees and wedges in the tunnel. The cars behind it plow into it sideways, exploding in a shower of debris. Metal shards and rods come sailing through my car, and I drop to the floor just in time to keep my head. I shove onto my hands and knees, swaying side to side while I crawl forward.

Heat flares when something explodes in the other part of the train. The fireball flares down the tunnel, and for a moment, set against it is a massive silhouette of a figure that could be a demon straight out of a storybook. From hulking shoulders spread massive wings crushed against the tunnel walls and roof because they're too big to fully unfurl. A long, black tail dangles away, and it carries some sort of hooked weapon on a pole. The beast vanishes among the flames, so close they lick the back of the car.

When they clear, the beast recedes in the distance, still standing despite the fury that just engulfed it. I'm quite thankful the train has not fully slowed. Is it the thing I saw in the gap between the cars? Fortunately, the tunnel curves, and the demonic beast leaves my sight.

I force myself across the length of the car and spill over the next gap.

The car seems designed with passengers in mind. Several booths line one side, and a single exit with hinged stairs features the opposite wall. I suspect this car must be where workers ride or maybe security. If there is a place Hazel would stop, this would be it, but she's not here. Leaving someone behind doesn't seem to mean much in this place, but there are seats here. Thank god, too, because I can't keep going.

I crash down at the edge of one of the booths. The exhaustion is overwhelming. I don't know if it's the blood loss talking, the fatigue of exertion, or the strain caused by prolonged pain, but my body's message to me seems quite clear: I hate you. It hurts absolutely everywhere. I try to focus on a single aching area, only for the pain from the others to blare. While I sit and pant, I weep.

The train continues to slow. How fast have we been going? Not that I mind leaving whatever was in the tunnel further behind, but we must have been going faster than a high-speed rail for it to take this long to stop.

My body shifts slightly at the final cessation of momentum. It's like my brain takes one step to the left in my head as well. There's a moment of disorientation, where my inner ears want to keep telling me I'm moving, but everything else says otherwise. Or vice versa. I don't really know.

I grunt like syrup glugging from a bottle, lean forward, and throw up between my legs. The convulsion of my ribs is agony, but it also feels like it's happening to my twin brother in another dimension or something. I gaze down into what I retched, as if I can read it like tea leaves. There's not much in the puddle I produce, just some spit and stringy phlegm. I haven't had anything to eat or drink for at least a full day now.

Has it been a full day? Is it still day?

After a moment, I force myself to get up. Really, I want to just go to sleep, but I have to get home. That's the only thing that matters now. I have to go find that kid and talk to him. Take him...somewhere. Where, I don't know anymore. And with Miela and Shadow Tommy both dead, I don't even know where to begin to find out. I'm so screwed.

Even though I made it this far, I am absolutely doomed.

I hate this place.

*****

Lie down and die. Turn to page 159.

I can't stop now. I can't. Turn to page 142.

There is one thing I know: I'm not athletic enough to keep running, but there's no way that stinking hole is safe. I'm going to need to stand my ground, and this might be my only chance to do it. With any luck, I'll be able to brag to my friends about having killed a giant flying shadow monster, not that anyone is going to believe me.

I drop into a crouch and grab the massive black urchin spine with both hands. When I touch it, that same cold feeling from before channels from my body into it, kind of like I am standing in the path of a giant air-conditioning vent. Though the spike looks smooth, it is gritty in texture, like coarse sandpaper. It is lighter than I expected, but sea urchin spines are hollow. Maybe whatever these formations are, they really are quite similar. Regardless, I heft the thing like a pike.

"What the hell do you think you're doing?" Shadow Tommy asks.

"I got this." Being armed gives me a strange sense of confidence, and I roll my shoulders back and set my jaw. I've seen *Braveheart* and know how to break a cavalry charge with a sharpened spike. So I jam the base of the spine into the rocks below me and drop into a bracing crouch.

"You've got a bunch of crazy." Shadow Tommy grabs a hold of my arm and tries to pull me toward the tunnel.

A woosh in the air, however, draws my eyes up. The flying shadow swoops, readying for its next dive. I lack any gentle and fast way to get Shadow Tommy out of harm's way, so I kick sideways and shove him down. He crashes to the ground with a grunt and a thud at the mouth of the icky tunnel. I wobble a little, my body getting colder by the moment. It's like the spine is sucking the heat out of me or something.

"You idiot," he says. "You fucking idiot!"

The beast crests, folds its wing, and begins its descent. Suddenly, I feel less like a vicious Scottish rebel and more like a piece of wet paper. My legs wobble, and my ankles threaten to give way.

"Let go of the spine," Shadow Tommy shouts. "It's absorbing your shadow!"

I nod numbly, but my hands aren't strong enough to let go. What seemed like sandpaper grip now feels like some sort of crazy glue. My arms shake, and I can't seem to get a proper breath. My head nods down, with my neck struggling to hold it back.

I raise it just in time for the open jaws, a black tongue, and what must be a hundred glistening teeth to snap shut on my temples.

***

You did not make the correct choice. Try again.
Turn to page 12.

I shuffle to the raised stairs and door to the outside. There's a panel on the wall with a lever. It is in the *up* position over the word "Close," and beneath it, it says "Open." I grit my teeth and pull the lever with the arm on my uninjured side. It resists for a moment but then gives with a whine. When it is thrown, the groan of unseen gears and mechanisms begins. The door grinds open, and the stairs shudder their way down in a faltering arc.

They settle into place with a creak, and a final *thunk* sounds with some sort of bolt or lock thrown to stabilize the descent. I nod, shuffle down, and step out onto a platform much like a subway station. The ground is paved with cobblestone, and large torches burn in sconces every fifteen feet or so. The ceiling here is vaulted, though, with graceful buttresses extending from columns to hold up the curved roof. Detailed reliefs are etched into the ceiling, portraying great cities and kingdoms.

I can see my breath. It's in thin clouds because I can't draw a full lungful, but goosebumps erupt over my whole body. It's not just blood loss. The temperature has dropped. It's like winter in Canada. Where the walls meet the floor, a thin layer of ice shines. I limp toward a massive staircase rising in front of me and groan. The stairs are steep, there are a lot of them, and swathes of black ice wait. Just what I needed—make it this far to fall and break my neck.

Why can't the damn kid just be waiting here? What's up there? Am I going to be expected to scour some massive city, asking for "Little Bit?"

Five steps up and my calves and thighs burn. I hold the banister with one hand and press my palm to my wound with the other. One step at a time. The cold deepens around me. I can't stop now. One foot at a time for a hundred steps before I stop counting. I'm too thirsty to sweat, which is awesome because my skin freezes to the rail if I hold it a fraction too long. If I could sweat, I would be coated in ice. Instead, my body feels hot and flushed. All my muscles shake.

A patch of ice in my path forces me to weave toward the center of the stairs. I clutch my arms to my chest, wanting to rub my biceps to warm them. But trying to do it angers the wound in my side. I pant with exhaustion, and each breath sends up a white cloud. Longer icicles seem to hang from everything the further I ascend. At the top, it looks like I'm entering some ancient ice cavern.

I retch again, this time nothing more than a dry heave, and I can't even spit at the end of it.

"Take your time," a leathery voice says.

In front of me is a stunningly massive chamber. It must be four or five times the size of a football stadium. with an impossibly tall domed ceiling which peaks at an opening to the sky. Ahead, there's a platform with benches—maybe every twenty yards in both directions around the ring—and then a rail. The barrier seems to run the whole length of the massive circle.

Beyond the rail, a massive cavern from which an ethereal blue rises. I know that glow. It's that of the sideways waterfall. My heartbeat accelerates at the thought of it, and my body instantly feels warmer. Almost euphoric.

I catch the rising giddiness and hold it back.

At the rail, beside a bench, stands the source of the voice. An old man with thin, gray hair and a weathered face—features from the World of Light. His skin is paper thin and looks as if brushing against him wrong may tear it. He wears long black robes, and his hands are covered by thick leather gloves.

On the bench sits a large shadow figure and a huge leather satchel, the kind they put loads of money within in movies. The black shadow figure wears a uniform so dark, it blends straight in with the shadow's skin. The shadow's hair is short-cropped, the face hard but feminine. I pick out a dark badge on her chest, and she appears to have some sort of holstered sidearm on her hip. Her clothing may be The Shadowland's version of a police uniform.

"We are in no rush," the robed man says. "But when you are able, please come close. This old voice lacks the endurance it once held in its youth."

I close my eyes. Light flashes on the inside of my eyelids. My head is pounding. The dehydration is getting to me.

"Don't think I'm going to get a whole lot better," I say, my voice a shadow of itself.

I try to straighten as best I can, but I feel like I'm ninety years old when I hobble forward, one hand to my side, the other steadying my hip. It's quite likely this individual met me at the top of the stairs specifically so I'd be exhausted when our interaction began.

"Come, to the rail," the robed man says.

I don't trust him, but I'm in no shape to fight, and I need to get a better look at the source of the glow. The light grows brighter, more engulfing while I approach. I tilt my gaze down into the massive pit, and there below me roils a massive ice flow. The current drives it in a spiral toward the outer edge, and a churning dome of ice slabs bubbles up at the centermost point.

The luminescence calls to me, and I yearn to throw myself over the rail. To immerse in its perfect radiance and become light. The pain in my side twinges and breaks my revelry. A little clearer, I remember before the train, when Miela talked about the caldera.

This must be the caldera.

"It's a volcano, isn't it?" I ask.

"An ice volcano," the man says. "The only one in the known universe."

"How's that even possible? That's not how volcanos work."

The robed man smiles.

"When I first came to The Shadowlands, I thought that so often about the things I found here. 'That is not how things work.'" He points to his palm for each word of the mock dialogue. "I thought this world was just a shadow of the World of Light. Shadow trees, shadow lakes, shadow sky."

The old man straightens his back in a way which makes him seem much taller, and he holds his hands out in a sweeping gesture to the caldera below.

"But then I learned that down in the flows below, there lives a shadow algae. Those algae feed off minerals in the water to reproduce, and in the process, they excrete an alcohol-like compound that lowers the freezing temperature of the water and bioluminescent microbial passengers. These microbes leach heat from the water, and then they metabolize the algae. This in turn drops the water temperature and increases the efficiency of the algae's reproduction. The microbes themselves appear to excrete a compound that is heavy enough to sink to the bottom of the caldera.

"Once there, I believe it reacts with a catalyst, and potential energy accumulates. That accumulation reaches critical levels, resulting in an eruption, spreading liquid ejecta for hundreds of miles, populating regional water flows with bioluminescence. Then, those waterflows eventually travel their way through underground caverns until they end up back at this caldera."

I stare blankly at the old man. He could be my geology teacher. But he could also be totally full of shit. I'm too tired to decide. The light in the cavern isn't the only thing which lights up this man's face. There's a passion there that, even in my near stupor, makes me want to listen.

"I don't fully understand this place yet," the man says. "But this is why I've traded so much to keep returning. This is why I studied Shadow Law and have taken onto my shoulders the burden of arbitrating the disputes between shadows and casters. And why I order the dispensation of justice to the guilty. It's a noble way to pay for the privilege of studying such majesty."

"Who are you?" I ask, though I already know.

The man looks to me and smiles. Then he looks over his shoulder and barks, "Officer Marbeth!"

The shadow officer rises from the bench. She clasps her hands to her sides and thrusts her shoulders back. In a voice whose true power is almost lost in the cavernous expanse of the caldera chamber, she belts out, "All will rise in the presence of The Judge and account for themselves under the witness of Libericia and The Thirteen. Though we are not in a court of Shadow Law, the Shadow Law holds court wherever one of its arbiters is present."

"I'm already standing." My side makes me wince, and the movement sends a bit of acid up from my stomach. A wooziness runs through me, and for a moment, my vision blurs. My peripheral sight is half gone. I take a little shuffling step to steady myself while I breathe in, good and slow.

"A mere formality," The Judge says. "All must be bade to rise at the start of an official proceeding and give their name for The Court."

"My name?" I ask.

"No one may stand anonymously under Libericia's witness, lest you face the justice of The Thirteen.

I hesitate, remembering the border crossing and the nickname I gave.

"Doom Boy," I say.

The Judge's face roils with condescension. "You dare give a false name to The Court?" His demeanor softens, and he suddenly seems much older. His shoulders droop a little, and it's almost as if he's added some liver spots to his complexion. "Do you see any thieves here? Confidence men? Do you see anyone other than myself and a trusted officer of the court?"

*****

No. It's really Doom Boy. Turn to page 147.

I'm sorry sir. My real name is Danny. Turn to page 153.

Maybe it's just me, but as stunning as the glow shimmering off everything is, it suddenly feels darker. More sinister. The Judge smiles a wicked grin. His teeth are tarnished and yellow. His lips are pale worms which look like they've not had blood flow in months. A sinking feeling fills my belly. He doesn't believe me.

Why did I think he would? My guts churn, and it's like some gnarled hand is squeezing my intestines. If I shit myself, will he have to reschedule this? Is that my road to salvation?

The Judge crosses his gloved hands, one on top of the other, in his lap. His voice is restrained, his tone measured. "Officer Marbeth, will you please check the name 'Doom Boy' against the border logs."

Officer Marbeth reaches into the bag and pulls out a thick, leatherbound book. The binding creaks when she opens it wide and fans through the pages. She supports the massive tome on one arm, gazing from the page to me and from me to the page. Then she turns the page to The Judge.

The Judge reaches inside his robes and pulls out a pair of small round spectacles with a wire frame. The light from the caldera shines off the lens so brightly, it's like they are made of the same radiance. He hooks one ear and the other, perching the glasses on the top of his nose, before he gazes down at the book.

My blood runs like ice. I don't know the law here and have no idea what it means to have called myself "Doom Boy" at the border. The clerk-thing told me to tell the truth, but Shadow Tommy told me to hide my name. Does The Judge know my real identity? Why did I listen to Shadow Tommy? He's dead, and here I am, trying not to shit myself. Am I going to prison? Worse? What do they do to you in The Shadowlands?

The Judge raises his chin to me. The caldera light shines from his glasses like his eyes themselves are calderas. Like they're about to erupt in an icy explosion and annihilate everything I am.

The Judge removes his spectacles.

"So be it. Let it be entered into the record that the subject of this inquiry has arrived in the charge of 'Doom Boy'."

Do what now?

The Judge looks to my feet.

"And now you must please rise as well."

"Um." I check around to make sure I'm still the only one here, other than The Judge and Officer Marbeth. "I am...risen?"

A ferocious light flares in The Judge's eyes. Old as he looks, I suspect he's as dangerous as anything else in The Shadowlands.

"Marbeth," he barks. "Give me the Hands of Attention."

The Judge holds his arms up like someone is pointing a gun at him. Marbeth reaches out and takes a hold of his palms. She slowly twists his wrists all the way around. The muscles and tendons in The Judge's hands go rigid while she does so. She spins the appendage a full 360 degrees. Then, she does it again.

And again.

The Judge's gloved hands pop off his wrists, revealing threaded screws at their bases. Marbeth bends and gently lays the hands inside the leather satchel. From that same bag, she removes a bundle wrapped in what looks like black silk. As delicately as one might unwrap a newborn, she opens the cloth and lifts out two new hands. These are gnarled and scabbed, scarred and blistered. Without so much as a blink, she attaches the new hands to The Judge's wrists, and upon the final tightening, they spring to life as if they've always been part of his body.

I look around again. Still the only one here. Am I doing something wrong? Should I have already found that kid?

"Okay..." I hold both hands out in a placating motion. "Now, if this is about finding Little Bit..."

"*Silence!*" The Judge roars. He spits on the floor, his face etched with disgust. The Judge rises and approaches me, testing the tightness of his wrists. "I do not expect to see the face of that child anywhere in The Shadowlands ever again."

"But I thought I was supposed to—"

"The problem with lackeys," the Judge growls, "is the ease with which they misunderstand even the simplest instructions, the most basic information. And the problem with casters is that they're so ignorant of The Shadowlands that they're all but impossible to communicate with."

Baffled, I try to follow The Judge's eyes. He's looking at the ground. At my feet? At my shadow?

I gasp softly.

Lower my arms.

The shadow's arms are clutched to its chest. They've been that way, even while mine were out, and they're not moving now.

That is not my shadow.

The Judge smirks, clearly aware I've realized the situation.

"I suppose you two haven't met," he says.

With the speed of a striking cobra, he jams the palms of the Hands of Attention to my chest. The jolt knocks me off my feet and sends me sailing backward. My ears ring, and my nose floods with a smell like ozone and burned meat. My heart pounds so hard, though, the newly bloomed agony where he seared my skin feels weirdly disembodied. I've had so much pain overwhelming my nerves and so much adrenaline pumping through my system, something in my brain isn't processing right.

It certainly doesn't understand the fact that my shadow is getting up from the floor and standing on its own. I try to sit up, but I feel like a turtle on its back. The Judge crosses his arms in front of what I thought was my shadow. It is no longer connected to me. How is it possible?

"Now that I have your attention," The Judge says, "identify yourself for the court."

"My name is Alexander," the shadow replies. "And I was once the shadow of a caster boy known in these lands as Little Bit."

I sit up and start to say, "What the—"

The Judge holds up a gnarled hand toward me, palm out. My mouth clamps shut. I won't survive being struck again. Of course, I don't know that I'm going to survive as it is. Meanwhile, The Judge lowers his hand and refocuses on the shadow.

"Do you know why you've been summoned here at great inconvenience?"

The shadow casts an accusatory glance at me and takes a step back.

"Because you believe I belong to The Shadower," Alexander says.

"I believe nothing. It is Shadow Law. And are you aware of your other crime?"

The shadow's face softens. Again, he looks to me, and the accusation is gone. Guilt swims in his eyes.

"I left The Shadowlands for the World of Light and attached myself to one of the Shadowless."

The Judge nods. "That is correct."

"Excuse me. What?" I say.

"I'm so, so sorry." Alexander walks over to me, holding his hands apart like he's carrying a big ball of apology and plans to hand it to me. He can't be more than twelve or thirteen.

The Judge gestures to Officer Marbeth, who makes her way closer to us while Alexander pleads.

"I thought it would help. Help *both* of us. I thought that if you had me, it would make you whole. That it would make you feel. I had no idea your brother and his shadow were involved in shadow dealing. I guess I should have figured out why you were Shadowless."

"Shadow dealing? Shadowless?" Maybe it's just the blood loss, trauma, starvation, thirst, exhaustion, and the insanity of all of this, but I'm struggling to process everything I'm taking in.

"You mean, you don't know? Your brother's shadow didn't tell you?"

"Tell me what?"

"Your brother sold you out. Sold your shadow years ago." Alexander's voice cracks while he implores.

It's so clear how young he is. If only I ever paid any attention to what my shadow looked like, maybe I would have seen it sooner.

"Why do you think you always had such a hard time caring about anything? You just want to coast away into video games and TV. It's because half of you just isn't there. There is no light in us if there is no dark. We can't soften anger into kindness without first feeling the anger. If you're Shadowless, you'll hardly feel anything, except when maybe something powerful enough reminds you of your old self for just a few moments. I thought maybe if you had me as your shadow—"

"But wait. Tommy's death devastated me," I say.

"Your brother's shadow didn't expect you to feel anything when he planned to kill him. When I showed up, he was already committed."

"But I never would have come here if I wasn't so wrecked. His shadow never would have been able to convince me."

"Yeah, I kind of screwed myself, huh?" Alexander says. "But I never meant to hurt anyone. Please. You can't let The Shadower take me."

Marbeth steps up behind Alexander and places her hands on his shoulders. Her grip is firm, and Alexander's face wrenches up when she squeezes.

"Perhaps now you understand his crime," The Judge says. "And that he is no part of you."

"Please," Alexander begs. "Please help me."

If my body were a separate being, I'm pretty sure it would be giving me both middle fingers right now. I'm so tired. Maybe I'm dead and haven't come to terms with it yet. I don't know if I have the strength to fight. Just want to be home. To see my parents again.

Still, right there: Marbeth's sidearm. It looks like some sort of cross between a taser and a flashlight. She is a shadow, though. Maybe it will bring her down? The Judge turns his back and shuffles toward the bench. Marbeth pivots her head to watch. If I'm going to do this, it's now or never. I press my hand to my side and take a deep breath.

*****

Take Marbeth's weapon. Turn to page 157.

Plead with The Judge. Turn to page 163.

The Judge smiles a wicked smile. Even in the ethereal light of the caldera, his teeth are tarnished and yellow, and the glow reflects off irregular patches, leaving the rest dark and pitted. His lips are pale worms which look like they have not had blood flow in months.

A sinking feeling fills my belly. I don't think this was the right call. No doubt, it's written all over my face too. Maybe I can call in sick and get them to reschedule. I cast a glance down into the caldera. The light calls to me. To my heart. Maybe it would be best if I just throw myself over right now.

The Judge crosses his gloved hands over his waist. His voice is restrained, his tone measured. "Officer Marbeth, will you please check the name 'Danny' against the border logs."

Officer Marbeth reaches into the bag and pulls out a thick, leatherbound book, just like the one the clerk-thing opened in the checkpoint. She licks her shadow thumb and brings it to the corner of the page, fanning through them until she stops. The binding creaks when she opens it wide and supports the massive tome on one arm. From the page to me and from me to the page she gazes, then turns the book to The Judge.

He reaches inside his robes and pulls out a pair of small round spectacles with a wire frame. The lenses flicker with the radiant caldera light, like TV static. He hooks one ear and the other, perching the glasses on the top of his nose. His eyes are lost behind the reflective sheen while he gazes down at the book. At what I know will be a picture of me.

My blood runs like ice. I don't know the law here. What will it mean that I called myself "Doom Boy" at the border? The clerk-thing told me to tell the truth, but Shadow Tommy told me to hide my name. Why did I listen? Why did I obey anything he said? Now he's dead, and here I am, at the end of this crazy quest he brought me on, trying not to shit myself. Am I going to prison? Worse? What do they do to you in The Shadowlands?

The Judge lets out a long exhale.

"Marbeth," he says. "Give me the Hands of Excoriation."

I don't know what that means, but I really don't like the way it sounds. My body has so little left, but I try to take a couple of discreet steps back. My hand has frozen to the blood soaked into my shirt over my ribs. My knees crackle, and little bits of ice scatter to the ground at my feet. My lips are frozen under layers of ice accumulating from the condensation of each breath.

Officer Marbeth opens the satchel on the bench. The Judge raises his arms toward her. The officer takes a hold of them and twists counterclockwise. His hands unscrew from his wrists like lightbulbs, and the loopiness returns to my mind. Lefty loosy, lefty loosy. When the gloved hands pop away, Marbeth sets them in the case and pulls out a bundle of black leather held shut by clasps.

With a kind of reverence, Marbeth dips her head while she undoes the buckles, and from the bundle she removes a new pair of hands for The Judge. Unlike the frailty of his face, these hands are young and unlined. Their palms are embedded with dozens of silver slivers. I don't know what they are exactly, but my skin crawls at the sight of them.

"You casters are all the same," the Judge says once the new hands have been attached. "You think the world is for you to do with as you please. You think of our home as an 'other place' to exploit for our unique resources."

The Judge gracefully wafts his new right hand down to the bench and runs his hand over the surface. His touch appears to be as gentle as one might caress a baby, but curling strands of the wood peel off underneath it. The strands fall away like fine shredded cheese. The silver slivers must be impossibly sharp to shave the surface so easily.

"Seriously, man, if it helps, I just want to not die," I say.

"Ah yes, control over death. To delay her grasp—the single most common and crass motive that brings you here," The Judge says.

"N-No," I stammer. "That's not what—"

"*Silence*," The Judge belts. He rises and draws his shoulders back.

His body grows taller and wider in the motion, and I suddenly wonder what is beneath the robe. I wouldn't be surprised if he ripped his shirt open like Superman and exploded with 800 tentacles.

"*Marbeth*," The Judge booms. "Bring the criminal closer."

"I'm sorry. I didn't know," I say.

The Judge's eyes widen with fury, and his jaw quivers.

"You claim the court officer at the checkpoint failed to inform you that the truth was expected?"

I got nothing. Really, I just keep making this worse.

"That's right," I say. "And he told me the shadows love the color orange and that you eat dung beetles and—"

The Judge holds his finger to my lips. He couldn't touch me more lightly and still be making contact, but my lips split right down the center, under the sharpness of the blades on his hand. The blood pours down my chin in rivulets and drips to my chest, where it freezes almost instantly.

"To lie to an official in The Shadowlands is a crime, but to be caught in a lie...that's a disgrace. Thankfully, the corrective touch of the law is gentle in its cruel kindness."

He runs his hand down my cheek, slicing right through the flesh in a dozen places. It hurts so bad, but it's strangely disembodied. Like it's happening to someone else who happens to be sharing my body.

"Lies are like skin," The Judge says softly. "You peel away the layers and see what really is when you get underneath."

He brings his hand down my jaw and across my throat. The cuts are so fine they sever my cells in half, though I don't get to really understand the perfection of their sharpness.

***

You chose wrong. You should have chosen No. It's really Doom
Boy. Turn to page 147.

There's not a whole lot I know about The Shadowlands. I don't know its history, its geography, its biology. All I've learned so far has been just enough to keep me from dying on the way here. However, there's something obvious: I've been manipulated and tricked into bringing this shadow-kid to a horrifying judge because someone bought him from a thief. There is no possible way this is fair, even if I have every right to be mad that I was the one dragged into it all.

I can't continue like this. It's my only chance.

I take my first step toward Marbeth. She looks back from The Judge to Alexander. I creep closer when she does, but my movement calls her attention to me.

The distance is small, though, and my next step brings me within arm's reach.

The problem is that damn wound in my side. I reach and yowl when the wound tears right back open. It's like someone's jamming fistfuls of needles between my ribs.

The great part is the yowl startles Marbeth. Her hands jolt off Alexander and jerk upward, even while my hand continues in its agonizing path. My grip closes on the handle of the weapon jutting from its holster, and Marbeth's reflexes give way to her training. Her hand dives toward the weapon too.

The weapon slides loose in my hand when hers reaches where it just was.

I have it. Holy crap, I have it. My momentum doesn't stop to celebrate, though. I take another step to keep my feet under me, but my upper body is moving faster than my lower because of the lunge. When I hit the ground sideways, wounded side up, my non-injured ribs crunch under my weight, and I bellow. It's a fight to keep conscious. My mind wants to shut the whole system down to stop feeling this.

I raise the weapon. There's a little plastic guard over the trigger, which I try to pop off with my thumb. It doesn't work. The thing is stuck on there good. I try to bring my other hand to the weapon to help, but my side hurts so bad, I can't even move it at all.

Marbeth rips the weapon from my grasp and removes the trigger guard with ease. The trigger *clicks*, but I don't see anything. The light flooding my eyes washes any coherent thoughts out of my head.

It's not like the light of the caldera, with its promises of euphoric bliss. Marbeth's light is searing and unbearable. I try to close my lids, but the light is so bright, it penetrates the thin barrier so intensely. It's like they're not even closed.

The fierce heat blooms a moment later when the liquid inside them boils the sockets. They burst, the searing goo running down my cheeks.

***

You chose wrong. You should have chosen Plead with The Judge.

Turn to page 163.

I lie down and close my eyes. My side hurts a little less this way, but my stomach still roils. My diaphragm convulses and sends a glut of bile straight up into my sinuses. I hack and retch even more, the pain racking my body horribly with every single spasm. It's a hideous cycle, and my body bucks and thrashes without my control. I'm seeing myself from the outside while my joints overextend.

My elbow cracks and bends forty-five degrees further than it should. My ankle jerks rigidly straight, and then my shinbone fractures and bursts through my skin. Tendons attached to my hips rip from their moorings and retreat to their muscles. At first, the agony seems distant, but then it grows brighter like the sun, burning me and tearing through.

My consciousness begins to break away from my body. But so is something else.

Something dark pulls away from my physical form—still breaking with further spasms—and crawls through the little puddle of vomit and back down the train car to the open door. The anguish becomes all-consuming when the largest convulsion yet breaks all my ribs on one side, and my throat attempts a long, deep scream.

Maybe I've been screaming since the convulsions started. Perhaps I've been screaming all my life. Maybe all I am now is that scream, endless in the experience of myself.

This was not a good idea.

***

Wrong choice. You should have chosen "I can't stop now. I can't." Turn to page 142.

I don't know what's going on, but something tells me I need to act fast. That is, after all, Tommy's voice. Even if he is a hallucination, the worst that will happen is I'll get into a coffin and feel like a batshit crazy idiot before I climb back out.

Nonetheless, I hesitate a moment and look over my shoulder. The gallery door is shut behind me. The bolt has been thrown. What the hell? Am I really being haunted? Could there be someone else in here with me? Is this all a prank? Air rattles through the vents, and I catch a thin echo of some sort of hymn they must have playing in the chapel.

Tommy points sharply to the coffin. Something about the urgency of the motion suggests it might be hard for him to speak.

I step toward it, and he moves back, clearing the way for me to climb on in. The coffin sends a chill through me, like I'm plunging into a pool in February. With Tommy's casket in the other room, I feel like I'm about to die as well.

Would my parents celebrate? When they got mad before this, they told me I was a lazy waste of space. "You're just going to rot away on the couch with your games," they would say. Would everyone fill with quiet relief that justice had been served? Or would they be saying, "If only Danny had been the only one who died"?

The real reason I'm doing this is because I do feel like I'm the one who deserves to be in the coffin. If I had just turned off the game and gone outside, I would have been there when he tripped or when he...Honestly, at the absolute worst, I would at least know what happened and if it could have been prevented.

The medical examiner told my parents Tommy drowned, but there was no sign he hit his head or somehow injured himself. He loved the water and was practically part dolphin. That's the thing about it, though. Who's to say what could happen to you when no one is looking.

When I'm all the way inside, I lie back and cross my arms, like I'm some movie vampire. The surface is oddly comfortable, and I wiggle a little to settle in. From inside, it doesn't quite feel like I'm in a coffin—most of the design that is "classically coffin" isn't visible from here. I could easily be lying in a padded trunk or in some strange, narrow bed with comfy rails on both sides, like a crib or bassinet.

What am I supposed to do now?

The lid slams down above me.

I attempt to shove the coffin open, but the lid will not budge. Is there a latch or something? I don't remember seeing one when I climbed in, but I also didn't think to check.

The darkness around me is total. I'm normally not claustrophobic, but I do not like this at all. When I give the lid a sharp shove, my hands jolt hard enough against the padding to send a bolt of pain through my wrists. But there is no give, whatsoever. I pound with the flat of my fist and jam my elbow against it.

Nothing.

"Help," I shout. "Help!"

I pound with both my fists and try with my knees as well. Should I attempt to punch my way out, like The Bride in that Tarantino movie? But I don't even know basic karate, let alone the fancy stuff. There's just so little room. My blows can't get any force, and my bonier parts start to hurt from the impact. My whole body thrashes, hitting the sides with my hips, trying to swing my shoulders up like I'm checking a hockey player. I push with all four of my limbs again and again.

My breath comes in harsh gasps. Am I just getting tired, or am I running out of air? Panic overwhelms me, and I lash everywhere until my muscles stop working altogether. Huge burning gulps of air sting my lungs.

A knocking sound enters my ears. Is it my heart? Am I dying?

Something splinters sharply beside me, and cold air rushes in.

The lid swings up, revealing Tommy's shadow against a reddish-gray sky. I suck in breath after breath. One of my hands grabs the rim of the coffin, and I press the other to my chest, as if that will somehow help me get enough air.

I sit up and look past Tommy's shadow. We're in some sort of wide-open space flat as a cornfield. Distant hills roll toward the horizon. The sun is high in the sky, but it's a dark, smoldering red, like a coal dying at the bottom of a barbeque. The wind blowing through is frigid, and my teeth chatter with the chill. I'm dressed for a funeral, not for...whatever this is.

The coffin itself no longer sits on a display platform. Now it rests atop a large flat stone. Around it stretches a field of what look to be black rocks, which all glisten in the light. They could be made of black ice or some sort of quartz, but they are all shaped like enormous sea urchins, their spikes jutting in all directions. Sharp enough to impale anyone who falls against them. Narrow pathways wind between them toward the horizon.

"What's happening? Where the hell am I?" I ask.

I turn to Shadow Tommy. He holds a prybar, which he tosses to the side.

Hesitating, I ask, "Who are you?"

"The simplest way to put it is that I'm your brother's shadow," Shadow Tommy says. "Or at least, I am his shadow as it exists in The Shadowlands."

"What the hell?"

When I look at Shadow Tommy with more focus, I can make him out a bit better. He isn't quite featureless, nor is he fully pitch-black. Subtle nuances of shade and color reveal traces of his characteristics, and though it's all blues and purples, much more of the brother I know is there. He extends his hand to me.

"Anything I tell you will sound crazy," Shadow Tommy says. "And we've got to get moving. It's not safe here."

*****

"Bullshit," I say. "I want answers." Turn to page 80.
Take his hand. "You'd better explain soon." Turn to page 9.

"Please," I rasp. I push myself to my feet and stagger back to the rail, where I take a hold. My hand flickers in the churning glow from the caldera. There's little strength in my voice—even less in my body—but there must be something I can say. With slow, shuffling steps, I limp along the rail, scooting my hand forward a couple of inches at a time. "Leave him be. Send me home. You can't do this."

The Judge raises an eyebrow at me. The light from the ice volcano seems brighter than before, and his whole pale face is lit like a reflection. The shine seems to smooth out his wrinkles and mute his features, and he almost reminds me of the clerk-thing at the checkpoint, except made of light instead of darkness.

"You presume to tell the law what it can and cannot do in its own domain?" The Judge asks.

"We're just kids," I say.

"A child from the World of Light has been killed by a shadow," The Judge says. "A shadow who has established himself with deals within The Shadowlands. This 'kid' as you call him—this displaced shadow—is at the center of a matter of some importance that left multiple influential brokers reputationally compromised. And even threatened my own standing. Had I more than tangentially intersected with this matter, I might not be here today."

"At least send me home," I say.

"You were not brought here through legal channels, so I see no reason you should be able to appeal to an officer of the court to help undo your foolishness."

The pain in my side is overwhelming. It's hard to draw a breath.

"But I'm dying."

"And you are free to do so as you see fit."

Anger runs through me. I want to lash out at something, but I have no strength. Even if I had some, I have no power. I'm just a kid too.

"It's just...This is unjust," I say.

"I did not realize you had been appointed a judge of The Shadowlands. Please, show me transcript of your enactment of the Great Trials. Show me your name in the Book of Meritous Shadow Patrons. At least provide the records of the proceedings you have adjudicated and the resulting verdicts."

I drop my eyes to the floor. To the lack of shadow at my feet. The Judge rubs his hands together impatiently.

"So I see," The Judge continues. "The simple matter is that no deal with you was broken."

I manage to draw a sharp breath. It clears my muddling head a little.

"A deal," I say. "I'll make a deal with you."

The Judge removes his glasses and cleans them with the corner of his robe before he tucks them into a hidden pocket.

"I am not without consideration for those who are sadly ignorant of the laws that govern the ground on which they stand. Let's see with whom we shall consider making a deal. Bring forth the reference."

The last sentence carries throughout the chamber despite its expanse. The light itself seems to amplify in sync with the speech. The lanterns around the stairs flicker, and movement draws my eyes down the path around the caldera.

On one side, a hulking form shuffles out as if from the wall, though likely through an opening concealed by the curve of the path. The bipedal shadow beast with huge wings folded on its back wears torn black pants and a top like some sort of medieval tunic. Its hands clench a long pole with a chain at one end, trailing back to a limping man being led by his neck. I only need to glimpse the salt and pepper hair and heavily lined face to know it's Journeyman looking far more beaten and exhausted than before.

"Now then." The Judge looks from me to Journeyman to Alexander. "Tell me what manner of caster to whom I am speaking."

*****

The final path is determined by the decisions made along the way.

I took the flower. I saw the lake. I pulled the cart.
Turn to page 166.

I took the flower. I did not see the lake. I pulled the cart.
Turn to page 170.

I took the flower. I saw the lake. I did not pull the cart.
Turn to page 174.

I took the flower. I did not see the lake. I did not pull the cart.
Turn to page 179.

I did not take a flower. I saw the lake. I pulled the cart.
Turn to page 185.

I did not take a flower. I did not see the lake. I pulled the cart.
Turn to page 189.

I did not take a flower. I saw the lake. I did not pull the cart.
Turn to page 193.

I did not take a flower. I did not see the lake. I did not pull the cart. Turn to page 197.

The beast behind Journeyman twists its shoulders back and drives him down before The Judge's feet.

"Officer Marbeth," The Judge says. "Bring me the Hands of Anointment."

Officer Marbeth returns to the satchel still on the bench. Alexander doesn't move an inch despite her absence, and in a moment, Marbeth has replaced The Judge's hands with a third pair. The left hand of this pair is a closed fist with a rusted-looking spike sticking from the extended thumb.

"In the light of Libericia and under the witness of The Thirteen, you are hereby bound to confess the truth of law," The Judge says.

He brings his new thumb to Journeyman's forehead and carves a curved symbol into the wrinkled flesh. Journeyman sucks breath through his teeth but makes no other sound, even while blood runs along the sides of his nose and into his eyes, forcing him to squeeze his lids shut. The blood continues down his cheeks and around his mouth, where it drip, drip, drips from his chin to the ground.

"Journeyman, you were companion to this caster on the journey from the border. Is he the type to observe Shadow Law?"

"He's so new here. He doesn't know—" Journeyman says, but The Judge presses his thumb harder against Journeyman's forehead and jerks it down his cheek. The old man's skin is gouged, and a flap hangs down, exposing his cheekbone.

"Immaterial. His level of experience is not in question, only your knowledge of his obedience to what he does understand of Shadow Law."

Journeyman nods. "When scorpion venom incapacitated me, this individual took the duty of pulling the cart from me and forced upon me an illegal rest."

The Judge shakes his head. I close my eyes in a long blink, and when I open them, I let them drop to the caldera. The surface reminds me of the way liquids spiral into a blender, except in reverse. It's like a hypnotist's wheel, and simply gazing into it shoves the pain in my side to the distant corners of my awareness. I struggle to focus.

"There is no greater cruelty than to break an obligation to Shadow Law, thinking it is mercy," The Judge says.

My stomach drops, and when I try to meet Journeyman's gaze—this man I only wanted to spare a little suffering—his eyes flit away. Blood spatters freely from his gushing cheek. I only wanted to help him. To be kind. How can it be cruel to be kind?

The Judge takes a shuffling step toward me.

"And you? Journeyman's said you crossed into The Shadowlands at Synoro from Black Rock Pass. That means you bridged the vertical lake." There's a bit of venom in his voice.

I look back to the caldera, to the luminescence. It calms me even while my heart wants to accelerate. I wish I could be just a little closer. It would help ease my nerves and soothe my wound. I'd be able to find the words.

"It's written all over your face," The Judge says. He turns to survey the caldera once again. "You'll never be able to leave. Not for good. You'll never stop yearning for that feeling."

He's right. Tears well in my eyes when I think about leaving this chamber. About taking my eyes away from this light. This is where I belong. I let go of the rail and stick my hands in my pockets. The rail is so cold it bites into my skin, but they feel restless instantly, so I pull them back out. The chrysanthemum I picked from Tommy's funeral arrangement falls to the ground and lands by my feet.

"Yet you can't be trusted to keep to Shadow Law, and even being Shadowless won't shield you from the desire for the Shadow Light." The Judge looks to Marbeth. He gives her a nod, and she returns it.

She goes back to the leather satchel of hands.

I bend down and pick up the chrysanthemum. Its simple petals are so soft in my fingers despite the fact they're numb from the cold. The purple color seems somehow untouched by the bluish light of the caldera. The Judge turns back to me when I pull myself up with the rail.

He sees what I hold and gasps softly. His hand immediately extends, palm up, but then falters. He withdraws it slowly and closes it into a fist.

"Do you know what you have there?" he whispers.

"A flower?"

"It hasn't even withered," The Judge says. "A whole day here and it's still pristine."

His arm trembles. It's clear he wants to reach out and take it. I don't know why the flower is so valuable, but it clearly is.

"It's yours if you just send me home and leave Alexander be," I say.

The Judge closes his eyes. They flick around behind the lids like he is dreaming. His Adam's apple bobs from a hard swallow.

"Officer Marbeth," he says.

The uniformed shadow lifts Alexander with one hand and glides toward me gracefully. She's much, much taller than I am. In fact, the closer she gets, the bigger she seems until she's a veritable giant on the platform. Marbeth takes a hold of the back of my neck with her other hand.

My feet are in the air. Officer Marbeth extends me over the rail, all while holding Alexander with her other arm. Such strength seems impossible, and yet it makes me realize I forgot to hold the proper awe for this place. The wound in my side explodes with pain when my weight shifts and hangs off my torso, but the light engulfs me from all sides. The platform no longer shields me from below. It's exquisite, and it turns down agony like a volume button.

"I'm sorry," Alexander says, his voice barely audible.

"Alas." The Judge opens his eyes. "Were I to take payment, I could not trust you to adhere to the bounds of our deal. If only you'd composed yourself with more discipline in your path through this world. Marbeth, you are the hands of my judgment."

Marbeth releases me. For a few brief moments, the wind rushes around me, and I'm fully suspended in light. Though I fall, it's as if I'm weightless. As if my spirit is perfectly buoyant. My eyes freeze when the intense cold of the ice caldera blasts me. My heart manages a single beat before it becomes a brittle, frigid thing.

THE END.

A bad feeling rises in my gut. Not only did I stand aside when Hazel killed Journeyman, but Alexander seems to have been the same shadow who led him to his current punishment. Will he separate me from my shadow? What can I tell him about my own life that will make me have value? That I stood up for my brother a couple of times?

I know Tommy didn't just drown—he *was* drowned—but standing here, the real truth strikes: If I had been out there with him, he would not have died.

I am guilty after all. The world wobbles around me. Some of it is my body just giving out. Some of it is the cold and the disorienting call of the light. But really, it's just a thick fog of guilt settling on my shoulders, even while I watch Marbeth give The Judge a new pair of hands.

Journeyman's lips move and say things about me I don't even catch. I try to listen, but I can't make out more than a word here and there. A droning buzz fills my ears. Haloes form around everything, and my vision blurs in and out. My focus wanders erratically, like I'm following a fly crawling across glass.

A splash bursts from the center point of the caldera, a fountain of liquid light that must be a hundred feet high. The Judge has his hands on Journeyman's face, and Journeyman wears a mask of blood and anguish. Icicles hanging from the rail break the caldera light into flashing rainbows. These shine onto Officer Marbeth when she steps behind The Judge with a thick, black towel, ready to wipe Journeyman's blood off whatever hands The Judge is wearing. The shifting beams flash onto the weapon on Marbeth's belt.

I don't want to fight, but running isn't an option. With this injury, I'd never make it down those steps, and I can't move faster than a broken walk. Either the beast who brought Journeyman or Officer Marbeth would be on me in a moment. Heck, The Judge could probably stalk me down, old as he is.

My hand moves practically of its own accord, creeping forward from my body toward the weapon. A little clasp is there to secure it in the holster, but it's not latched. I tell myself to stop, but my hand won't listen. At the back of my mind, there isn't a voice, but I have the impression of someone speaking. Of Miela speaking.

There are no words, but the anger is clear. I remember the strange shadow worm she set into my chest. Is this her doing? Or am I just trying to justify something really desperate? It could be both. Or neither. In the end, I suppose it doesn't really matter because my fingers spread and pinch the weapon.

Officer Marbeth visibly stiffens. I jerk it from the holster and let myself fall backward, even as Marbeth twists to look at where she just sensed contact. The weapon is shaped kind of like a flashlight, and there's a switch underneath a plastic cover. Marbeth's eyes widen. Her right foot takes a step forward and to the side, and her weight begins to shift into a full pivot.

I flail my other hand against the trigger cover, grabbing with frantic strength. My grip lands. The cover clicks off and swings back, and I break it off at the hinge. Marbeth's foot raises, and her weight shifts forward to dive at me. The Judge too turns, his head halfway around, one eye looking straight at me from its corner.

With a click, the trigger depresses.

The world goes white. Pure, dazzling white. The kind you see when you get hit in the back of the head. The kind they show in movies when a nuclear bomb detonates.

My eyes tear up, but the light is so intense, the tears instantly evaporate. As does the liquid on the surface of my eyes.

My vision does not come back.

Marbeth crashes into the railing beside me, her momentum having already been committed to the dive. The Judge bellows, and I push myself to my feet. He's right there. I can knock him over the railing. Barrel forward with my shoulder out like a football player and charge into the empty sky of my blindness.

My shoulder hits something. Someone. Their weight flies backward, even as I keep driving forward. They grunt when they hit the rail, and I keep on shoving them back. An upper body shifts and is gone. The scream which follows is young—a child's.

I slump forward against the railing, barely not tumbling over myself.

Someone scuffs against the platform behind me.

The Judge's voice is gruff, strained.

"The Shadower won't be happy," he says.

I think he's talking to me, but he doesn't sound like he is speaking in my direction.

"Arrest him, Officer Marbeth."

There's a slight pause and more shuffling from yet another location. After a meaty thud, I suspect Officer Marbeth has fallen.

"I'm hurt," Marbeth says. "Badly. I can't see."

"I can't see either," The Judge admits. "And I'm wearing the wrong hands."

I want to laugh, but all I can manage is a wheezy chuckle. It's agonizing, of course, but my body is miles away now. My weight slides down the rail. It's more comfortable not to hold my muscles firm enough to keep myself upright. Or to brace me.

I slump onto my side. Try to picture myself at the edge of the caldera. Rolling over into the radiance. With my eyes destroyed, I will have to rely on my dreams.

The cold ground feels like it's part of me. My temperature is dropping, my heart is slow, and my breaths are shallow. The Judge and Marbeth might be able to hope for rescue. Journeyman and the beast who held him should still be here, but they have not made a sound. The beast doesn't seem to have responded to The Judge's call. Maybe Journeyman just wants to die and go home. With any luck, they'll stumble blindly in a newly dark world, and The Judge will never see the shadows he loves.

For my part, I'm content to stay where I am. To let myself dissipate. To become less than shadow. My hand brushes against my hip. Against the mouth of my pocket. There's something there. Something soft. I pinch it between my fingers and bring it close to my face. Try to hold it up to my eye, as if that will fix the thing broken in my retina. But I do catch the slightest whiff of something floral.

The flower I took from Tommy's funeral display.

I press it to my seared cheek. Of course, I can't see it, but I looked so closely at that display, I can imagine it perfectly. My final thoughts pour over the last beautiful thing I ever saw.

THE END.

The Judge adjusts his robes and examines the seam where his hands screw into his wrists. He scrapes a bit of ice that has clung to the edge of the...attachments, and he raps his knuckle on the railing. Journeyman winces.

"You understand the penalties for lying before the court?"

"I do," Journeyman says.

The Judge takes a step forward. In the radiance of the caldera, he looks ten feet tall. The shadows resting on his shoulders are stark and shifting. The cloth of his robes flutters in a frigid gust of air which rushes out from the icy peaks. A deep rumble far beneath us vibrates through everything.

"You understand that your history of protecting caster children against their obligations to The Shadowlands leaves your truth before the court in question?"

"I do," Journeyman says.

The light from the basin shifts and swells. The Judge and I both cast a glance past the rail. A jet from the center sprays up a hundred feet and arcs back down. I remember the night of upward rain, the vertical lake, and the sideways waterfall. The Judge seems lost in thought himself, the smallest smile on the corners of his lips.

He turns his attention back to Journeyman.

"And that should I believe for a moment that you are distorting the truth to protect this caster child, I will use the Hands of Scouring to hollow you out until nothing but the truth of your testimony remains?"

Journeyman closes his eyes.

"I do."

A slight sound draws my attention to the stairwell down to the train platform. The steps themselves are empty. The black ice across the top seems to have spread the whole width of the passage. Is something there? The Judge and Journeyman don't seem to have noticed at all. The beast who brought Journeyman and Officer Marbeth both have their attention focused on the caldera.

"When you took this caster up the road from the border, you suffered injuries to your legs."

"This is true."

The Judge places one of his hands on Journeyman's shoulder. Journeyman looks down and away. This is like pulling the cart with the scorpion stings swelling up and oozing. This is not a testimony. This is part of his punishment. The Judge's hand squeezes. Something electric seems to pass from The Judge's hands to Journeyman. The Hands of Attention, weren't they?

"You have attested that the caster intended to alleviate your burden despite the rules of your punishment but chose to refrain."

"This is also true."

"You also have attested that when you encountered one of the children who blames you for their forced departure from Gissu, this caster allowed her to take vengeance upon you rather than protect you?"

Journeyman narrows his eyes and glares at me. Is he about to lie? Should I have helped him? I would want revenge if he had let someone murder me.

Another scuff from the stairs...

I look over just in time to witness something dark rising just above the level of the top stair.

A long breath escapes Journeyman's lips.

He opens his mouth to speak.

The caldera rumbles again. This time, the shudder it sends through everything is strong enough for icicles to break from their moorings and crash down to shatter. They crumble all around the platform, but hundreds of larger ones free themselves from the vaulted dome roof and drop over the caldera. It's like a glowing rain of streaking shards.

Marbeth and the beast are momentarily transfixed, tracing the falling ice upward toward the roof, perhaps to see if more might fall. The shadow coming from the stairs rises into a crouching run. It is Hazel, and she holds a dagger in one hand and a shadow blade in the other. She glides forward, like a ghost among all the clatter of ice cracking into fragments.

Hope fills me when I realize there is someone who can help. Someone who can intervene. The Judge hasn't seen her yet, and she's practically upon his back. I want to cheer.

Then Hazel shoves The Judge aside and buries her dagger straight through Journeyman's eye. She jerks the blade out— white goo, blood, and brain matter clinging to the knife—and jams it in through his other eye before his body can collapse.

"Stop in the name of the court," The Judge says, slumped against the rail.

Hazel turns on him, and Marbeth strides toward her back. The officer snaps her wrist out, and a baton extends like it's part of her arm. She snaps it again, and a series of blades like straight razors snap out from the central shaft. The beast, too, has seen what is happening and approaches with its chain-pole.

I don't have much strength left, but I press one hand against my wound and fling myself toward Officer Marbeth. My hand grabs a hold of the weapon on her belt. It doesn't slide out of the holster. Rather, it jams against the leather, but the sudden pull of my weight throws off Marbeth's balance. She falls sideways over me, straight into the path of the beast.

Her momentum carries her into a roll, and the weapon slips from the holster. I don't know how to use it or exactly what it will do, but it looks like a flashlight, down to a switch on the side. A little plastic cover protects the switch, and I crack it back hard enough, it breaks off at the hinge.

Hazel sees the weapon in my hand.

"Close your eyes before you use it," she says.

She closes her own and turns away.

I do what she says when I press my switch.

Even through closed eyes, the light is dazzling. It's so intense that, when I open them back up, the whole world flashes in a haze of rainbow splotches. I sit up, finding Hazel at my side, sliding my arm over her shoulder. My side screams at me when she hoists me to my feet, and we stagger forward. I glance back to our captors.

The Judge moves slowly in a daze. He presses his fingers to his eyes and rocks a little on the ground. I wonder if he can see anything.

Marbeth and the beast both take my breath away. They're withered to a shell of their former selves. Both look like grapes left on the vine. Just past them, I spot Alexander in the same state. A twinge hits my heart on that, but he is a huge part of why I'm in this mess to begin with.

I look across all three again.

"Are they dead?"

"Not dead," Hazel says. "But they'll be down a while. We have to hurry, though. I don't think this place is as stable as they expected."

As if on cue, the caldera rumbles again, and a fresh jet sprays up. This one nearly reaches the level of the platform.

"I can't," I say. "I can't keep going."

And it's true. Now The Judge is done and his help subdued, the adrenaline pushing me this last mile dissipates rapidly. My vitality is pouring out of my side...and fast.

Hazel stops. "There is one way," she says, her voice reluctant.

"I'm listening."

"You can take me as your shadow," she offers.

"Do what now?"

"Well, Alexander latched onto you and hid without your permission. He simply changed his form to look as much like your shadow as he could manage. And since you didn't even think to pay attention, he got away with it. He was never really your shadow, though. However, we can choose to join together, and if we do, we'll be sent to the World of Light."

"And what do you get out of this?"

Hazel reaches inside her clothes and holds something out in her palm. Its purple color is stunning against her hand, even amidst all the light from the caldera. It takes me a second to realize where it came from. It's the flower I took from Tommy's funeral arrangement.

"I took this from your pocket just now. A single petal had fallen out on the train, and I'd hoped you had more. Shadows here would fight each other to hold something like this from the World of Light. This...this is delicate. Lush. I don't want to keep living in a place where it's astonishing to find a single flower. Where food and water that has real taste withers and rots in hours. I know you saw the lake because I see how you look at the light. Right now, that seems like all the beauty in the world, so amazing you want to become it, but that's just because of how it stands against the rest of this place."

Around us, as if the volcano itself wants me to stay, the light flares, and a torrent of liquid jets up far higher than the platform upon which we stand. The light itself is engulfing, and my heart surges with the thrill of being illuminated by it.

Nonetheless, I look back at the flower. My vision is dim and hazy, but even still, I can see just how nuanced its texture and tones are. At the same time, I think of Tommy's funeral. Of Mom and Dad. No matter what our life is like if I return, I won't be shadowless, so maybe I can be someone they'll be proud of. If not, I'll do my best to try.

I meet Hazel's eyes. "Will you...be me?"

"Maybe? I don't really know," she says. "This will be my first rodeo."

THE END.

A low rumble sounds from the caldera below. The railing beside me vibrates, and bits of icicle fall away, shattering on the ground around our feet with a sound like tinkling bells. Officer Marbeth leans over the railing and peers down below. The beast clenches its hands around the pole which brought in Journeyman.

For his part, Journeyman looks grim, sad. I can't help but pity him. He did, after all, lose his son by the sounds of it, and this place can't be anything but torment from what I have seen. Literally. It's actually the law, as far as I can tell.

As part of that, The Judge asks Marbeth for something he calls the Hands of Anointment, and Marbeth breaks her attention away from the caldera. The intensifying swells of the unnatural radiance almost seem to diminish where her body edges. The bright light makes her smaller. Is that the effect of all light? My eyes fall to the weapon at her waist. From here, it looks more like a flashlight than a firearm.

I try to bring my attention back to Journeyman and The Judge, but it's so hard to focus enough to pull together whole sentences, especially with The Judge going on about Libericia and The Thirteen. He's warning Journeyman of consequences, but before I can listen enough to confirm, I notice Alexander inching toward me.

Another rumble from the caldera draws Marbeth back to the edge, and the beast sniffs the air cautiously, amid a sprinkle of ice dust drifting down from the ceiling. Are we nearing an eruption? The rumble continues in a low steady churn.

Alexander whispers, "Do you have anything of value?"

I don't know. Do I? Slowly, I pat myself down until I reach my pockets. No wallet or keys since I was just going to a funeral with Mom and Dad. The only thing I have is my phone. Is that valuable? Even if it still had juice—which I sorely doubt it does— there would be no way to charge the thing, and I don't think The Shadowlands has a satellite network.

Nonetheless, I pull the phone out of my pocket, immediately groaning when I notice the massive web of cracks covering the screen. A small, purple object falls to the ground. I frown and furrow my brow, pressing my free hand to my side. When I kneel to brace my wound, a kind of numbness settles into my body. I set my phone on the platform and pick up the purple thing.

It's the flower I took from Tommy's funeral arrangement. I hold it up in the caldera's radiance to examine it more closely.

Alexander gasps. "Is that..."

His shadow hand darts down and snatches the flower from my fingers. With quick steps, he trots past me toward the beast at the base of the stairway up. I try to rise, but my exhaustion and injury keeps me on my knees. Alexander thrusts the flower to the beast, and the huge creature's eyes widen. It reaches out when Alexander lays the flower in its palm, turns, and disappears up the stairs.

What the hell just happened?

Behind me, The Judge gives a *tsk, tsk, tsk*. He shakes his head at me somberly.

"You knew well enough not to break our laws by offering respite to Journeyman," The Judge says. "But you don't understand them."

"How am I supposed to?" I ask. "Everyone's been lying to me."

"The Shadowlands itself never lies," The Judge says. "And you've not listened. You saw the endlessness of The Boiled Sea. You walked alongside the sideways waterfall and had to have tasted of its light. You crossed the plains of the upward rain and saw our emissary's delight. This land can be harsh and cruel, and as such, beauty here can compel. That flower, for better or for worse, is rarer here than a gem in a place where things that depend on the World of Light wither in hours. Chrysanthemum's symbolize death and mourning. They exist on the edge of The Shadowlands already, and they last longer here than any other flower. My servant will be punished for its distraction but also understood."

A shudder runs through me. Exhaustion is breaking the last bits of will holding upright my bones. None of this matters, does it?

The Judge himself shrugs and looks to the officer. "Marbeth, bring me the Hands of Restoration."

Marbeth retrieves from the satchel a pair of hands holding an enormous bone needle with a long black thread hanging from it. My eyes widen.

"Um, I don't think that's necessary…"

The Judge nods absently, as if expecting the objection, while Marbeth attaches his new hands. When they're locked in place, he gives both wrists a flex, sweeping them in a little sideways "s". He presses his lips together.

"Your shadow friend who brought you here didn't want you to be able to return just by dying, like most casters here, so he kept you planted in The Shadowlands by removing a bit of your heart's shadow and replacing it with a bit of his."

"No," I say. "He didn't add anything. He just…" But I trail off.

Of course, he lied about that too.

"When I remove it and repair the tear, you'll return to the World of Light when your body gives up here in The Shadowlands."

"So, I'll just go home?"

The Judge nods.

"And you'll go back to being Shadowless," he says.

"I won't get my shadow back?"

"Pssht," The Judge scoffs. "Your shadow is long gone. Transferred property. I wouldn't know where to begin to look, even if there were legal recourse for its retrieval."

A wave of weakness rushes through me, and a fresh pressure surge launches a fount from the center of the volcano. It's not an eruption, but my bones grind. I set one palm to the ground to brace myself. It seems I'm out of time.

"All right. Let's just get this done."

The Judge approaches with the bone needle extended. Is it sharp? Really, really sharp? Because it looks like something you would see in a natural history museum and wonder how people used such a blunt tool.

The needle draws close to my skin, and a strange pulling sensation floods the muscles over my ribs. Marbeth steps behind me and tears my collar down, exposing the area, revealing the skin and flesh beneath are curling back from an opening between my ribs. When the needle reaches it, there's nothing to push through. There's a dark channel into my body the needle vanishes within, causing the same pulling sensation to spread across my back.

The needle passes between my shoulder blade and my spine, and the thread disappears inside. With his free hand, The Judge reaches into the gap and tugs something. From the hole, he draws a long, black thread.

The shadow worm Miela put into me.

"All sorts of folk been meddling in here." The Judge chuckles. "But it's like they say. Other than the deals you make, nothing's really yours in The Shadowlands, not even your body."

The needle passes in and out of me. Each time, something in my chest seems to tighten. To pull together. After seven passes, The Judge stops. He raises and appraises his work.

"There," he says. "Good as new, wouldn't you say?"

Officer Marbeth moves beside him and rests her hand on her chin before giving a small nod. I feel like a piece of found art being judged by a couple of critics.

Marbeth steps forward and removes her weapon. It's shaped like a flashlight, but she grips it sideways. She draws her hand across her body, the butt of the weapon toward me. With a lightning pivot, the weapon flashes down, the butt striking me across the temple. My skull cracks an instant before the world becomes blackness.

My eyes open.

The blackness is still there. Total.

I'm lying on something soft. When I thrash out with my arms and legs, something heavy above me jerks up and then back down with a bang. I put my hands and knees to it and push out with more coordination. A panel longer than my whole body swings up and to the side, and I sit up, finding myself in the funeral home showroom coffin. Trained by the prolonged pain, my hands seek out the wound on my side, only to find it completely healed. There's not even a scar.

Did it really happen?

My head feels like I've got the mother of all hangovers, and I wait a few moments for my thoughts to collect. I think back to the needle. The Judge. I take a deep breath. My body seems healthy and strong.

Unsure what else to do, I hoist myself out of the coffin and shuffle to the showroom door. I take the handle, certain I'll be locked inside, but the knob turns without a problem.

Through the front doors, it's clearly night. One or more streetlights cast their glow to the road below. Their glow is a sickly yellow I can't help but compare to the caldera's radiance.

Was there a caldera? I don't really know. But I clearly missed the rest of the funeral. Do Mom and Dad think I am missing? Or do they just figure I wandered off to hide, to escape the pain I caused for everyone?

I thumb the lock of the funeral home front door. An alarm system starts its warning buzz, but I don't have a code to shut it off. Nor does it really matter. If the police come and get me, I'll tell them I fell asleep in a coffin. Maybe I'll get in trouble. Perhaps they'll give me a pass because of Tommy. What else can I tell them? What else can I do to help myself?

I step out into the cool night air, standing a moment and stretching my arms. Am I really home? Does it matter where I've been?

I look down at my feet when I step into the streetlight's glow. They meet the pavement, but the light is not broken. I'm throwing no shadow. How odd, but then, is it really? If it is odd, does it matter?

After everything, I would like to just get home and sit myself on the couch. Play a few rounds of a shooter or something. Zone out to whatever show is "recommended."

THE END.

"Marbeth," The Judge says. "Bring me the Hands of Scouring."

Journeyman's eyes widen. What little color he has drains from his face, and his eyes follow Marbeth's path to the satchel. Just then, a low rumble rises from the caldera. Marbeth pauses while she rummages and looks out over the volcano. The light from it intensifies, and as it does so, Officer Marbeth's own physical self seems to recede just a little.

She may be shadow made solid, but it seems like bright light might diminish her. The beast, too, seems a little off-kilter. Its own shadow body almost blurs at the edges. Is that something I can use to fight back? If there's a flare from the ice caldera, will that be a moment of weakness?

"You won't need those hands." Journeyman brings his eyes back to The Judge. "I've got nothing to hide."

The Judge sighs. "I'm sure that's true. But the Law must counterbalance our understanding of your sympathies."

I only have to look at their dynamic for an instant. Even if Journeyman defended me, perhaps for giving him rest while pulling the cart, The Judge will now allow anything but a forced confession. I look from the pair to the beast and Alexander. The beast seems to have lost interest in the proceedings and approaches the rail while the pole it holds dangles from its hand. Its long curving tail flits nervously while it surveys the ice flow. Meanwhile, Alexander is slowly inching to the side. He casts glances to the stairs from which the beast and Journeyman emerged.

A clatter, barely audible over the rumble from the volcano, pulls my attention to the stairs. For a moment, I think I catch a glimpse of movement close to the steps, as if someone or something is crawling low, just out of sight. A surge of adrenaline gives me a bit of strength, like pieces are moving together in a way that will give me some sort of opportunity. I'm too weak to run or to fight, but maybe with the right advantage, I can even the playing field just long enough to take a hostage, negotiate, or something.

"When you escorted this caster and the accompanying court officer," The Judge says, "according to your account, you were injured by obsidian scorpions."

"That is true," Journeyman says.

"And the caster attempted to intervene in your punishment by relieving you of your duties?"

I frown. You could certainly put it that way, but I was only trying to show a little kindness. Maybe to prove my strength a bit.

"This is true as well. The officer of the court warned him of the rules to which I was bound at that point."

"And did this caster show proper deference to the court?" The Judge asks.

Journeyman shakes his head. "No."

"And yet, despite this claim of mercy, when the shadows with whom you'd previously associated came to exact their vengeance, this caster made no attempt to intervene?"

A chill beyond the frigid air around us courses through my belly. I don't like where this line of questioning is going.

"No attempt whatsoever," Journeyman says, scowling at me.

"Now, wait a second." I don't know what else to say, but the look The Judge shoots me is so sharp, all thoughts flee.

"So, when it's a clear matter of law and you've been duly warned, you disregard the rule of the land. But when it suits your own safety, your mercy ends?" The Judge snaps.

"That's not how it happened," I insist, but I don't know how else to put it.

The Judge's baleful glare is overwhelming. I've been through too much and am far too injured. Shouldn't a court let me recover before forcing me to fight for myself? It's not fair.

Another clatter comes from the stairs behind me, and The Judge, Journeyman, and I turn.

Hazel sprints from the passageway. She holds a regular dagger in one hand and a shadow blade in the other—no doubt the same weapons from the train. In several deft steps, she bounds over and around ice patches, landing directly between Journeyman and The Judge.

The beast roars and raises its pole over its head. Officer Marbeth's hand drops to her belt, and she grabs at her weapon. Hazel drives the dagger upward into the bottom of Journeyman's jaw. The blade slides right in, and he makes a sort of *gluck* sound when his tongue is jammed to the roof of his mouth, even while the weapon continues its path into his brain through his palette. His body erupts into violent convulsions, and his eyes roll back.

With the shadow blade, she slashes out backward and cuts The Judge across his belly. The blade cuts deep into his side at the same height of his navel and exits from the similar spot on the opposite side. An explosion of blood erupts and splashes across the floor. The beast lurches toward us, and Marbeth raises her flashlight-shaped weapon. The Judge's wound widens when his back arches, and a large number of gore-coated round objects tumble from his abdomen.

Organs, I assume for a second, but they don't look quite right.

Alexander lurches toward the stairs when the beast passes him. Marbeth clicks a plastic casing off the trigger of her weapon and closes her eyes. The beast launches into the air to tackle Hazel—and maybe me—with its arms outstretched and its wings fully extended. I close my eyes and brace for the potential impact.

A stunningly bright light erupts around us. Even with my eyes closed, it's agonizing to perceive. The flash is gone in an instant, but when I open my eyes, everything is splotchy and hazy with rainbows.

The Judge has collapsed to the floor. One of the objects which fell out of him has come to a stop beside my knee. My vision is too messed up to be sure, but it appears to be some sort of skull. An animal skull maybe. I don't have a chance to think about it, though, because I also see Hazel.

Hazel's body has shriveled like a worm lost in the sun, like some mummy dredged from a deep tomb. Beyond her, Alexander and the beast were also caught in the weapon's blast. The beast still bears some semblance of its strength and attempts to bring itself upright, staggering and falling back to the ground.

Alexander's mouth opens and closes, and he draws slow breaths. His eyes have been burned from his skull.

Officer Marbeth alone remains unscathed. She surveys the ruin with a grim gaze before settling on me. Her face writhes with fury. I want to tell her I didn't cause this, that none of it is my doing, but I doubt it matters.

"You have a choice," she says through a clenched jaw. "I can crush your skull right now, or you can dive into the caldera."

I force myself to my feet, even though what's left of my strength seems to be pouring straight out of the wound in my side. The blood covering my hands is nothing compared to the light. That radiance. I remember the lake. The sideways waterfall. That desire to touch the glow itself.

My body turns to the rail, and I clench it with both hands. My side is agony when I raise one leg to the bar, but I don't care. If I can't make it home, at least I'll feel at ease in the light. As one with the light.

Over the side I roll myself, letting out one last, slow breath as I fall into that frigid abyss.

THE END.

Before The Judge can say anything further to Journeyman, Alexander steps forward. The beast behind him snarls and raises its pole, but The Judge holds up a staying hand. The light welling from the caldera pulsates. A shudder seems to ripple through the whole mountain.

"Your honor." Alexander rubs his hands together. "I can clear this up right now."

The Judge puts on a patronizing smile. "Oh, can you now?"

Officer Marbeth turns to face him, and the beast comes closer, looming over my short-term shadow. At any moment, it's going to reach out and rip him in half or maybe throw him against the icicles hanging from where the wall meets the edge of the dome. At the same time, the radiance below seems to ripple. The icicles all shimmer. The gleam catches in the coat of ice on the railing and the black ice patches on the platform. It's like sparkle trapped in glass. I want to gaze at it, but the flare dies down.

Things seem so much darker.

"You want to know about this caster," Alexander says, "and I've been attached to him long enough to tell you everything you need. He didn't even know I was there, so he hid nothing."

Fear slithers through my belly, colder than the deepening chill in the air. I cross my arms over my chest and suppress a shiver, which causes the wound in my ribs to throb.

"And why would I believe stolen property?" The Judge scoffs.

"Because I'd like to make a deal," Alexander says.

The Judge's posture adjusts. He smiles slightly and clasps his hands at his waist. What the hell? As if he hasn't caused me enough trouble, he's going to sell me out again? Does he have no shame?

"And what do you propose?"

"I'm here because you recently lost a shadow thief," Alexander says.

The Judge's shoulders roll back. Sharp anger floods his eyes. Beside him, Marbeth seems to surge in size.

"I and the Court have lost nothing. We do not possess thieves," The Judge growls.

"The Shadower, then—"

The Judge raises both hands so they're crossed at the wrists and slashes them down and away from each other. "The Court stands apart from The Shadower. How *dare* you impugn officers of the law."

"But," Alexanders says, "but I thought—"

"You did *not* think," The Judge says. "And now, I'm afraid you've left me in an awkward position."

The Judge looks over to Marbeth and gives a slight nod with a regretful expression in his eyes. Marbeth steps forward and takes Alexander by the biceps.

"The Court cannot be seen as being in the debt of any entity, lest our impartiality be subject to question," The Judge says heavily. "As such, we must make a show of independence."

Marbeth lifts Alexander from the ground. His feet kick while they rise, but the officer's arms have grown too long for him to swing his heels back and make contact. He looks more childlike than ever before.

"Please, don't hurt him." I don't know why I don't want to see him hurt. Really, I owe nothing to him, and he has caused me unimaginable trouble. But yet, he was also a part of me, if only for a while, and I don't know if I can see him any other way. Frantically, I search my pockets for something to offer The Judge, but I find nothing but my phone, its battery dead and its screen hopelessly cracked.

Nonetheless, I hold it out desperately.

The Judge takes one glance at it and gives me a sad chuckle.

"And here you would openly bribe the court, even as it asserts its authority on the dishonest?"

"No, I—"

"I know you interfered with Journeyman's toils out on the Black Rock Road. I know you bore witness to the barrier lake despite your guide warning you against. I know that before you arrived here, you let your brother die because you couldn't care enough to get off your couch. To let your mind pay attention to your world."

"I didn't know," I say. "I didn't even know I was Shadowless."

"You just didn't care," The Judge says.

"I *did* care. There were times—"

"And yet, when your brother needed help, he thought the only way was to sell your shadow out from under you rather than asking."

His words are knives, and I don't know how to block their stabs. The Judge makes a flicking motion with his wrist. Marbeth lifts Alexander over her head and flings him into the caldera. He screams while he falls, but his voice withers almost instantly. The light around him intensifies, and his body shrivels.

It might be that the base of the caldera has grown so bright I have to squint, but it looks like Alexander vanishes altogether right before he hits the flow.

The Judge watches the ice surge over the rail for a moment before he turns back to me.

"He did have something of a point," The Judge says to Officer Marbeth. "The Court is always in need of servants who can venture into the World of Light, and we've had some serious disruptions of late."

"I agree, your honor," Officer Marbeth says.

Then, The Judge turns back to me.

"As it happens, it seems you're about to die," The Judge says.

As if on cue, my legs wobble beneath me. The moment swept me away with adrenaline, but now that surge is gone. The fatigue consumes me from the inside out. My temples pulse like the light in the caldera. I feel kind of faint.

"And unlike most casters, your shadow friend who brought you here altered your shadow so you wouldn't just kill yourself to return home. We can fix that," The Judge says. "Or we can let you die here and now and throw your remains into the volcano as well."

"Please, sir," I whisper through gritted teeth. I press my hand against the wound in my side and try to take a real breath.

"Sir?" The Judge says.

"Your honor," I say softly. It's not even a whisper. It's the shadow of one.

The Judge clasps his hands behind his back, looking pleased.

"Outstanding," he says. "I'll consider this your consent. I will have Officer Marbeth take on new duties as your shadow, and you'll find yourself returned to your home once you die."

"And that's it?" I ask.

"For the most part," The Judge says. "Except that your relationship with Officer Marbeth will be different than with your original shadow or with Alexander. With them, you were the agent of decision. With the court's representative, you will be but a passenger in your body."

I don't have time to respond.

Officer Marbeth steps up to me from behind and wraps her arms around me. All at once, the boundary between me and her becomes blurred, and it's like I'm being pushed out of my own form. Her shadow absorbs into me and then slides across the floor. Her will is like a hurricane battering against the distant corners of my skull, and before I know it, it's like I'm a painting looking in at the space that was myself.

The Judge chuckles. "A fine day for justice," he says.

Then he turns to the rail and takes hold of it, looking out into the light of the caldera.

THE END

The beast behind Journeyman twists its shoulders back and drives him down before The Judge's feet.

"Officer Marbeth," The Judge says. "Bring me the Hands of Anointment."

Officer Marbeth returns to the satchel still on the bench. Alexander doesn't move an inch despite her absence, and in a moment, Marbeth has replaced The Judge's hands with a third pair. The left hand of this pair is a closed fist with a rusted-looking spike sticking from the extended thumb.

"In the light of Libericia and under the witness of The Thirteen, you are hereby bound to confess the truth of law," The Judge says.

He brings his new thumb to Journeyman's forehead and carves a curved symbol into the wrinkled flesh. Journeyman sucks breath through his teeth but makes no other sound, even when blood runs along the sides of his nose and into his eyes, forcing him to squeeze his lids shut. The blood continues down his cheeks and around his mouth, where it drips, drip, drips from his chin to the ground.

"Journeyman, you were companion to this caster on the journey from the border. Is he the type to observe Shadow Law?"

Journeyman nods. "When I was injured, this caster was struck by sympathy for my pain and intended to relieve my burden, as is the way of so many casters ignorant of Shadow Law. However, when my court-appointed courier apprised him of my punishment, he set aside the desire of the light, and my punishment continued unabated."

The Judge presses his palms together and looks at me appraisingly.

"And as I understand, this caster arrived in The Shadowlands via The Black Rock Road at Synoro?"

Journeyman nods again but does not elaborate.

The Judge takes a step toward me. "That means you bridged the barrier through the path beneath the lake."

My throat is parched. I remember how Shadow Tommy warned me not to look. How I insisted. My eyes fight my will to return to the caldera and take in the light. To guzzle it until it fills me. I give a slight raise and drop of my chin.

"And did you look upon the lake?" The Judge has a strange hunger in his voice, an energy in his poise.

I can't help but turn toward the caldera. To revel in how much I want to be in that light. Even when I turn back to The Judge, who looks like he's about to spring onto me and start stabbing me or something, I feel like I should throw myself over the railing, to be one with the glow. This is my place. I know it. If I am allowed to stay, than there will always be a chance I can become part of this light among all the shadow.

"I wish I could see that light again for the first time," The Judge says. "But to have seen it is to know one of the depths of The Shadowland's beauty."

"It was amazing," I say, my voice hoarse.

"There is so much more," The Judge says. "Places like no other. Stories unlike any you've ever heard."

My heart pounds, and my head is woozy. I can't tell if I'm about to collapse from weakness or if it's the light consuming my thoughts.

"Let me stay," I whisper.

The Judge looks to Officer Marbeth. "Bring me the Hands of Comfort."

From the satchel, Marbeth retrieves a new set of hands. These are a warm yellow and covered in fuzzy gloves. They almost seem to glow against the ethereal light of the caldera – indeed, as Marbeth draws near, the air around us seems to warm. A crisp scent almost like an incense fills the air. Methodically, she replaces The Judge's hands, at which point The Judge flexes his new fingers and places them on my biceps.

The warmth runs through my whole body, and all my pain diminishes.

"I would offer you a choice," The Judge says. "If you have something of value, you may purchase your way back to the Light, or you may buy permission to stay here as a free apprentice of the court."

There's nothing in my pockets, not even my phone—the only thing I really valued at home. I don't even know what The Judge would find valuable.

With a slow shake of my head, I say, "I have nothing to trade."

The Judge smiles somberly. "A shame, but not without remedy. The Courts don't allow poverty to preclude service." He brings his hand to my wounded side. "Your body is damaged. We will accept, as payment, the source of your suffering."

My head swims. It's hard to swallow.

The heat in his hand intensifies. Becomes searing. My whole world goes white with a kind of suffering fire unlike anything I've ever known. The entire side of my chest erupts. I try to scream, but it's like my lungs aren't even there. My mouth is just open and useless, my tongue trying to belt out the sound of my agony.

And then, it is gone.

The Judge's hand is gone too. The yellow glove pulls away. The robed man steps back while I survey my own body.

My shirt is half gone, and so is the flesh and bone underneath. In its place is a metal-plated surface, except the metal has many joints, which allow me a stiff sort of movement. My ribs and the muscles over them are gone. Something mechanical ticks inside my chest when my lungs inflate.

"With your gift of flesh and our gift of machine, our pact is sealed." The Judge turns his back and begins to walk away.

"What about Alexander?" I ask.

"He has never been the property of the court," The Judge says. "He will be given to the one to whom he is owed."

I don't have a choice but to understand. Something in the back of my mind compels me to accept it—the same compulsion

I felt from Miela's strange shadow worm but much stronger. I wonder if her influence on me died with her.

Whatever The Judge has done is more potent. For a moment, I want to feel sorry for Alexander, but an angry righteousness comes from that same place of compulsion. The sense that he deserves his punishment. That the right to rebel was never his to begin with.

"Now, come," The Judge says. "I will take you to the capital courthouse at Chhoya, and you will begin your study."

My feet obey his word without consulting my mind, and Officer Marbeth drags Alexander behind her. I want to look back and see what happens to Journeyman, but my neck won't obey. What happened to Hazel? The thoughts fragment before they form. I try to think of Dad. Of Mom. Their faces won't even come.

At the same time, from within the steel cage The Judge has built around my heart, the certainty of why they won't come emerges: I've not been given permission.

And that's okay. I watch the light of the caldera while we walk. I'd jump in, but that too would not be permitted.

THE END

The radiance of the caldera swells below, shimmering in the icicles hanging over everything and gleaming off the ice-coated railing. The shadows in the room retract and expand. The pulse is steady and regular, and my failing breathing synchs up with it. It's oddly calming, and my thoughts start to wander, even though the conversation before me is life and death.

I picture the funeral display around Tommy's casket and all those myriad flowers, wishing I had, in fact, taken one. The light from the ice volcano pulls at my heart because it is lovely and soothing, but it's not the same as holding something in your hands that is tangible. Real. Beautiful, like the flower.

I break my thoughts away and turn them back to Journeyman and The Judge. The Judge apparently has asked Officer Marbeth to change out his hands. I don't know what this type is. The palms are covered with a swath of sharp needles at different angles.

I press a hand to my wounded side and pull it away. It's not actively bleeding, but blood seems to have recently oozed from the gash. My palm in the ethereal light is not red but black, like I'm bleeding shadow. A lightheadedness washes over me.

With the new hands on, The Judge flexes his needle flingers and playfully jabs Journeyman in the cheek with one.

"I know your history of flouting the court to protect a child." The Judge twirls the needle around in Journeyman's cheek.

Journeyman sucks a breath between his teeth. "I understand your mistrust, but though that may be Little Bit's shadow, this kid isn't Little Bit."

"It's like what the casters say about us shadows," The Judge says. "Like one, like all."

With each of his words, The Judge slides a needle on a different finger into Journeyman's teeth. The man clenches his fists, and the tendons in his neck all go taut. He fights not to jerk away. The Judge withdraws all the needles. Little drops of blood pop out on Journeyman's face where they entered.

"And like the truth about shadows," Journeyman says, "every caster is different. I appreciated his compassion to help, and I appreciated that when told the law he did not."

"I suppose a willingness to obey is a trait I can respect," The Judge says grudgingly.

He turns to Alexander, approaching the shadow who once trailed at my feet. I try not to look at The Judge's hands while he wiggles his needle-covered fingers, so I divert my gaze to the light trapped in the railing ice and listen to the rumble from the caldera when a flow jets upward.

In all the shifting light, I can hardly recognize anyone's features. I can't even tell how Alexander is reacting to The Judge's approach. His face is as uniform to me as the clerk-thing at the border checkpoint. My eyes blur, and my pulse throbs behind them. My breath rattles in my throat. My muscles spasm, and I drop to my knees, bracing myself on the ground with one hand.

The Judge glances at me and scoffs before returning his attention to Alexander. I'm dying, but it doesn't matter. Maybe I would die here no matter what I did—if I stayed, if I went home. Perhaps I'd just be on the couch, playing games and zoning out. The light from the caldera swells again, and a fresh jet launches up from the center. But even the strange intoxication of the light I felt in the tunnel to the vertical lake fails to stir me now.

"You've been watching this caster longer than any of us," The Judge says to Alexander, with a flourish of needles. "Have you seen him show any character that gives him value to The Shadowlands or the World of Light?"

Alexander looks at me. The Judge slides one of the needles into the joint of his neck and shoulder. Alexander whimpers at the jab, but I can't make out his expression. His face is still an undistinguishable blob.

"He doesn't understand the beauty of The Shadowlands," Alexander says. "He didn't even risk seeing the vertical lake, even though he'd been transfixed by the water's glow moments before in the tunnel."

The Judge nods gravely. He withdraws the needles from Alexander's collar and presses several more between the ribs on the right side of his chest.

"And what waits for him in the World of Light?"

Alexander sobs at the pain and groans thickly. He shakes his head.

"Nothing. His mother and father loathe him and the way he sits on the couch or in his room every day, staring at video games or the TV."

The Judge laughs once, harshly.

"Transfixed by light but cares little for the beauty of the Shadow Light."

"He doesn't have friends," Alexander continues. "Or the ones he does, he's never met. He belongs to nothing and to no one."

"I see," The Judge says.

He turns and pores over me with crossed arms and wrists bent out, those needles all splayed to the sides, away from his biceps. His head cocks sideways, and he mutters to himself. Around us, the caldera luminescence swells, and a heavy rumble churns. Things fracture everywhere with sharp snaps, and for a moment, it seems as if the whole dome is going to come down.

Instead, huge icicles, exploding in showers of ice pebbles. We all wince and close our eyes when the spray stings our faces.

If I had strength, this would be the moment to make my escape.

If I could think of any way out of this, this would be the opportunity to pursue that route.

I open my eyes. The Judge's are still closed. Marbeth has covered her own with the inside of her arm. The beast has shrouded its head with its wings, and Alexander has dropped to his knees, both arms over his head.

This is my chance.

I've got nothing.

I take a deep breath, which pains every fiber of my being.

The Judge opens his eyes and smiles.

"*Tsk, tsk.* Even now, there's nothing within you. Still, I understand how people from the World of Light loathe death. How they fear to enter endless shadow." The Judge holds both his hands in the air in front of them, fingers pointed up. For a moment, I think he's about to slap down all those needles onto me, but instead, he says, "Marbeth, bring me the Hands of Reinforcement."

Officer Marbeth digs through the satchel and removes a pair of oddly gnarled hands, whose fingers almost look like tree roots. She removes the needle hands from The Judge's wrists and affixes the new pair. When they lock in place, The Judge rolls his wrists and gives me a small smile.

"There is room for those who want to live to serve the court in special ways." The Judge steps closer.

He bends over and places one hand on my head and the other on the small of my back.

A strange spasm lurches through my body, like a massive jolt of electricity. I convulse and barely manage to keep myself on all fours. My knees and elbows bear all my weight. My side is a ragged thing of flaring agony, but then a stiff ripple runs through my chest. My skin seems to tighten on me and pull outward. A squelching sound worms into my ears, and flesh rips and tears, twists and stretches.

Something extending from the back of my neck forces my head level, and it affixes to my skull. My hips and shoulders lock into place, and my biceps and thighs become rigid, like they're made of metal. When I look down as best I can, my arms have taken on a strange swirling texture. Like woodgrain.

The caldera surges again with its brilliance. For certain, my arms *are* made of wood. Some blackish wood with deep grain patterns. No doubt, my legs are the same. Something above me, large and round, extends away from my back in all directions, leaving me largely cloaked in its shadow.

"Perfect," The Judge says. He kneels and bends sideways to look me in the eyes. "You'll make a fine table for the Court offices. Marbeth will see to it that you're kept fed. Don't worry. Without a shadow, what's left of the bit of caring you got from Alexander's stay will be gone altogether soon."

I try to scream, but my chest won't expand enough to allow me the needed volume of air. My vocal cords don't work anymore either. Perhaps they, too, have transformed. I don't know because I can't see myself or move. It's not that much different than being on the couch, playing games. If the past me entered, I'd probably set a controller and a drink down on myself. Maybe kick my feet up. I wouldn't bother to wipe up the crumbs or think twice about leaving a mark.

THE END.

For more of The Shadowlands, watch for news about the upcoming re-release of *The Neverborn Thief.*

For more fun-filled deaths, please check out the rest of the

Try Not to Die series.

Available on Amazon.

Out Now:

At Grandma's House
In Brightside
In the Pandemic
In the Wizard's Tower
Wild West
At Ghostland
At Dethfest
Back at Grandma's House
On Slashtag
In a Dark Fairy Tale
At the Meadow Spire Mall
The Shadowlands
In This Damned House
In Arcranium
Escaping the Cult

In the Works:

Super High
In Brownsville
In the UK
In the Tournament of Mortem
In Area 51
In Hollow 2
In a Prison Riot
At Desperation House
In a Video Game
By Your Own Hand
Between the Worlds
25 Perfect Days
Hanging with the Homies
With many more soon to be announced

How Did You Do?

We hope you enjoyed the book and wouldn't mind giving us a little feedback. Thank you so much for your support.

Scan the QR code to answer a few questions about your reading experience.

Thanks!

Thank you, dear reader, so much for taking the time to find this book and to play your way through its pages. Bringing my work to readers is literally the single best thing about doing any of this. I hope you enjoyed your experience in The Shadowlands, and if you haven't already, I hope you're willing to venture there again in *The Neverborn Thief*. This world exists for you.

Thank you to Mark Tullius. I would be lying if I didn't admit that I'd been secretly hoping I'd get an invite to write a *Try Not to Die* book. But that's also like hoping I'll win the lottery. I was absolutely floored when it happened. Thank you so much for checking out my work, doing me the honor of letting me create an entry for this series, and for letting that entry focus in on The Shadowlands. I have a special love for that dark place, and I'm so thrilled that I got to revisit it from new and exciting angles.

Thanks as well to Tim McWhorter, who brought *The Neverborn Thief* into the world. While *Try Not to Die* is meant to stand on its own as a story, it is also something of a sequel to my first horror-fantasy novel. If Olive-Ridley Press had not taken the chance of bringing Neverborn to readers, I never would have had the faith in the title to also pitch its world as my idea for a *Try Not to Die*.

`An additional thanks must go to Patrick Reuman. Though this title doesn't build off my Wicked House titles directly, it is absolutely my success with *The Mobius Door* and *Gollitok* that brought me here. And I owe a good chunk of that success to Patrick's deep caring for his press and the authors he publishes. He does small press publishing right.

Thanks, too, to the amazing folks I've met through Wicked House—most notably Blaine Daigle, MJ Mars, Will Gray, and Duncan Ralston. I do not intend to sleight any of the others, but these four are the ones I've spoken with the most, especially on a craft level. They are an incredible community to be a part of, and they're among my favorite friends.

Of course, thanks as well to Jon Cohn. In the most immediate sense, his *Try Not to Die on Slashtag* title was my roadmap for how to write a *Try Not to Die* book. And all the conversations we've had about game making, writing, and even The Shadowlands itself have been an enormous help and support. I've never had the chance to engage in concerted collaboration until working with Jon on our game project, and it's been an amazing process I've learned enormously through.

Of course, all those authors and others—Andrew Van Wey, Angel Van Atta, Ben Young, Edmund Stone, Megan Stockton, Jay Bower, Debra Castaneda, and so many more—y'all are incredible folk to be part of a community with.

I've also got to thank Tyler Kraha. He's been a sounding board and support for so many different projects I've worked on, including being an invaluable alpha reader who offers amazing feedback. He's also just plain and simple a great friend, whose support in other ways has been essential to overcoming some of life's worst challenges.

The last thanks I'll offer here is to my family—Amber, my wife, Gillian and Elliott, Alex and Ashton, my mom, dad, and Tiffany; heck, even Fern Dog the Ferninator, Hazel the Kitty, and Snakey. The family is why this work happens. They drive everything I do. They are my everything.

I'll end here knowing there's so many folks I've forgotten, so many steps I need to appreciate for me to be where I am. Please, everyone accept this blanket thank you, thank you, thank you.

About the Author

Andrew Najberg is the author of the best-selling (#1 US Horror Amazon) novels *The Mobius Door* (Wicked House Publishing, 2023) and *Gollitok* (Wicked House Publishing, 2023), as well as *The Neverborn Thief* (Olive-Ridley Press, 2024), the forthcoming collection of short fiction *In Those Fading Stars* (Crystal Lake Publishing, 2024) and the forthcoming novel *Extinction Dream* (Wicked House Publishing, 2025). His short fiction has appeared in *Fusion Fragment, Khoreo, Translunar Travelers Lounge, Utopia Science Fiction, Prose Online, Psychopomp Review, Solar Press Horror Anthology,* and more.

He also has published the poetry collection the *The Goats Have Taken Over the Barracks* (Finishing Line Press, 2021), and the chapbook *Easy to Lose* (Finishing Line Press 2007). His book *Fighting Fermi* is forthcoming through Walnut Street

Books. His poems have appeared in dozens of journals online and in print, including *North American Review, Asheville Poetry Review, Another Chicago Magazine, Yemassee, Cimarron Review, Louisville Review,* and *Good River Review.* He was the winner of a 2010 AWP Intro award in poetry, and the 2022 Brain Mills Press poetry month grand prize winner.

Currently, he teaches creative writing, Japanese literature, rhetoric and composition, and honors seminars in the humanities for the University of Tennessee at Chattanooga where he also serves as the director of programming for the honors residential college.

Download Your Free Copy

Includes the first two chapters and one or two death scenes

from each of the first 14 books in the *Try Not to Die* series.

Try Not to Die: For Free

Try to survive the first chapter of Books 1–14

Download both samplers for free.